"What makes you think you'll end up pregnant?"

Slade's voice was stone cold. Bronwen stole a glance at him and didn't like what she saw.

"I—I didn't mean that," she stammered.

"Really? How interesting. Does that mean you've decided I'm a reformed character? Or that you're not the sort of woman you think I fancy in bed?"

"I—*neither*." Bronwen couldn't go on. She didn't really know what she'd meant, except that she was certain he hadn't reformed. And she wished she was anywhere but alone with him.

"Is that so?" Slade turned to face her. "In that case, I guess it has to be yourself you don't trust, doesn't it?"

Kay Gregory grew up in England, but moved to Canada as a teenager. She now lives in Vancouver with her husband and the family dog. The couple's two sons and Kay's innumerable jobs have often provided background for her books. Now that she is writing Harlequin romance novels, Kay thinks she has at last found a job that she won't find necessary to change.

Books by Kay Gregory

HARLEQUIN ROMANCE
3016—A PERFECT BEAST
3058—IMPULSIVE BUTTERFLY
3082—AMBER AND AMETHYST
3152—YESTERDAY'S WEDDING
3206—BREAKING THE ICE
3243—AFTER THE ROSES

HARLEQUIN PRESENTS
1352—THE MUSIC OF LOVE

AN IMPOSSIBLE KIND OF MAN
Kay Gregory

Harlequin Books

TORONTO • NEW YORK • LONDON
AMSTERDAM • PARIS • SYDNEY • HAMBURG
STOCKHOLM • ATHENS • TOKYO • MILAN
MADRID • WARSAW • BUDAPEST • AUCKLAND

TO LOIS SADDLETON
Who has been my friend since I first came to
Canada, and has always known how to make
me laugh.

ISBN 0-373-03330-3

AN IMPOSSIBLE KIND OF MAN

Copyright © 1992 by Kay Gregory.

Printed in U.S.A.

CHAPTER ONE

BRONWEN, who was suffering from jet lag, slept in that day, so she didn't find out she was dead until early in the afternoon.

She had woken to the sound of two men shouting at each other in the street below. When her bleary gaze fell on peeling sunflower-spattered wallpaper she winced and shut her eyes again briefly.

Last night she had been too weary to care where she slept, just so long as it didn't cost much. Now she gradually became aware that the hotel she had wound up in was of the type that would most likely be labeled seedy.

She sighed, pushed herself out of bed and, after dressing in yesterday's clean but tired traveling clothes, headed downstairs in pursuit of a very late breakfast.

It was while she was hunched over a grease-smeared table in the run-down café next door that she happened to glance at the paper abandoned by the previous diner—and caught sight of a short paragraph on the back page which read, "Mystery Girl Killed in Taxi Tragedy."

She took a bite of her buttered toast, noted with vague surprise that it wasn't cold and crisp, as breakfast toast was served at her home in Wales, and ran her eyes idly over the news item.

It stated that a young woman newly arrived from Britain had been killed yesterday on Vancouver's Pender Street when the taxi she had been a passenger in had hit a bus. The two drivers and the bus passengers had survived. The young woman had been rushed to the hospital, but had died a few hours later.

Her name was Bronwen Evans.

The toast slipped out of her fingers and landed face-down on the table. She blinked, and reread the piece again from the beginning.

"But I'm not dead," she muttered out loud, just as a waitress came by to replenish her cup.

"Glad to hear it, dear," said the untidy middle-aged woman, giving Bronwen a lopsided smile. "Can't say the same for all my customers, though." She threw a disgusted glance at a man who was drooped over a table across the aisle with his eyes closed, and his nose almost buried in his soup.

Bronwen looked up, startled. "Oh. I didn't mean . . ." She pointed at the article. "I was just reading this bit in the paper. I think it means me, because my taxi *was* in a collision yesterday. It was a car we hit, though, not a bus."

The waitress skimmed her eye swiftly over the page. "Don't make much sense to me," she agreed. "They're supposed to inform next of kin first. You'd think they'd at least inform the body."

Bronwen choked, then stopped chuckling abruptly. "Next of kin——" she gulped. "Oh, Lord. Michael. If he sees a paper . . ." She jumped up, almost spilling the full cup of coffee, threw some money on the table and scurried toward the door.

"Hey," called the waitress. "Hey, miss, you've left too much . . ."

But Bronwen wasn't listening. She hadn't time to sort out the intricacies of the unfamiliar currency. She had to get back to the hospital and Michael. It was bad enough that he was lying there injured. He didn't need the added shock of his sister's death. Not, she

thought wryly as she hurried to catch the bus she had
been told would take her directly to her destination,
that he had seemed overly concerned about her welfare
these past eight years.

It was hard to believe it had been that long since
he and Slade had left Pontglas so suddenly—in the
process breaking her parents' hearts. After Michael's
departure they had both aged rapidly, and when illness
had struck three years later neither of them had had
the will to fight back. They'd died within two weeks
of each other, leaving Bronwen the sole owner of the
variety shop they had dreamed of handing over to
their son.

Before his parents' death Michael had written once
or twice to let them know he was all right and happy
enough living in Canada. But in the five years that
had passed since then he hadn't written at all. That
hadn't surprised Bronwen much. Michael was like
that. Thoughtless, irresponsible, but never deliberately unkind.

When the long-distance call had come from the
pleasant-voiced stranger, to say that her brother had
been stabbed in a street fight, that hadn't entirely surprised her either. But she had packed her bags immediately, left the shop in the care of a retired couple
who sometimes helped her out, and taken the first
possible plane to Vancouver.

The bus pulled up, and she glanced anxiously at her
watch—then realized that the time of day didn't
matter. What *did* matter was that Michael, now well
on the road to recovery, shouldn't see the paper before
she reached him.

He was propped up in bed, leering around a thermometer at a pretty black-haired nurse. Bronwen sank
back against the doorframe, limp with relief. Even

Michael wouldn't be making eyes at nurses if he'd just heard that his sister had been killed.

"Bron!" he exclaimed as the young woman removed the thermometer and he caught sight of his white-faced visitor. "What's the matter? You look worse than I do."

Bronwen glanced down at her green tweed skirt and sweater. They were neat enough, if a little warm for this mild May afternoon. So Michael must be referring to her face.

"I'm fine," she said quickly. "I had a bit of a shock, that's all." She pulled a chair up beside his bed and began to tell him about the newspaper article. When she had finished Michael threw back his dark head and laughed.

"Well, I'm damned," he said, wincing because laughing strained his stitches. "I wonder how in the world they got that story."

"I don't know at all. I'll have to go down to the emergency department and get them to sort it out. I suppose that's where the muddle started."

Michael grinned. "You'll give them quite a turn. I bet it's not every day that one of their bodies comes back to haunt them."

"Mmm," agreed Bronwen, who wasn't totally sure she found the subject of her own demise amusing. "Speaking of bodies, you look much better today, Michael. They'll be sending you home soon, I imagine."

"I hope so."

She eyed him severely. "And there will be no more of this foolish fighting."

"Of course not," he replied, looking reproachful. "It wasn't *my* fault, you know."

"No," said his sister dryly. "It never is."

As far as she could remember, nothing had ever been Michael's fault. When he got into trouble, according to his version, it was always someone else's doing. Usually Slade's. And then he had wondered why her parents had disapproved of his friendship with the older boy.

She shook her head, came firmly back to the present, and told her brother that, as everything seemed to be all right with him for the moment, she supposed she ought to go down to Emergency to straighten out the confusion that would undoubtedly be stirred up by her remarkably improved state of health.

"I'll see you this evening," she added—and then wondered why she'd even bothered. Michael's wandering gaze was already directed hopefully at a passing aide.

He's twenty-nine years old, she thought resignedly. Three years older than I am, and he still has the mind of a teenager. She sighed. Possibly the hormones too.

She brushed a strand of bright red hair out of her eyes and swung briskly into the corridor. But she had only taken a couple of steps when she realized that the man in the white shirt coming toward her had stopped suddenly, blocking her path so she couldn't move.

"Excuse me." She stepped to the side, still seeing only a well-cut shirt covering a well-muscled masculine chest.

"Bronwen?" The voice was familiar. Deep, crisp, oddly sensuous, with a faint North American overlay that only partly disguised the low British drawl that she remembered.

She looked up, very slowly. "Slade," she whispered, feeling the color drain from her face. When her eyes finally met the cobalt blue stare that she had never quite forgotten she saw that he too had turned white—although how anyone could look white under his naturally golden skin tone was beyond her.

"Bronwen Evans," he said huskily, putting out a hand to touch her, as though he wanted to assure himself that she was real. "Bronwen Evans. But you're—good Lord."

Shock began to wear off, and Bronwen felt the first stirrings of an old indignation. "I could say the same," she said curtly. "I would have preferred it if *you* had disappeared from Michael's life too. And what's so surprising about my being here? I am his sister, remember."

"Yes," he agreed, his voice neutral now. "And I assure you I haven't disappeared. You, on the other hand, are not dead."

"Thank you," said Bronwen. "I didn't think I was, but it's a great relief to have the matter confirmed."

She made to pass him, but at once his hand curled around her elbow, and she saw the blue eyes spark dangerously. As always when she allowed herself to think about Slade, she couldn't help noting that his mane of Viking blond hair was the perfect complement to those striking eyes. Striking was the operative word at the moment, she decided. He looked as though he wasn't sure whether he wanted to laugh or slap her. She stepped back quickly when he let her go, and his long mouth curved in a thin smile.

"Shy little Bronwen," he murmured. "How times change. You've acquired a sharp tongue since last we met." His tone had been drawling, speculative, but it hardened suddenly. "Why, Bronwen?"

"Why what?"

"Why aren't you pleased to see me? I thought we were friends."

Friends? They had never been friends. Acquaintances perhaps, but she had never spoken to him much when he'd used to go around with Michael. He had been so flamboyant, always the center of attention, and shy little Bronwen hadn't really liked that much. She'd much preferred quiet Lloyd Morgan at the time. Besides, her parents hadn't approved of Slade. They, mistakenly in Bronwen's opinion, had thought it was his influence that was causing their son to lose interest in his family and the shop. She'd had no wish to add to their worries.

"We weren't exactly friends," she said evenly. "And I'm not especially pleased to see you, if you must know. But that doesn't matter, does it? You came to visit Michael, I imagine." Her smile was cool.

"I came to break the news to Michael that you were dead. Before someone else did." Now his eyes reminded her of chipped ice. "But obviously that won't be necessary. At the moment I'm much more interested in finding out what you're doing, standing here on two solid, very sensibly clad feet, when it was reliably reported in the paper that you were decently laid out in the morgue."

"*Unreliably* reported. Sorry to be such a disappointment." She was irritated, not only by his tone, but also by the unflattering reference to her flat shoes. She was also irritated to discover that she cared. His opinion of her shoes shouldn't matter.

"Oh, you're not a disappointment," he said grimly. "A shock, certainly, as well as something of an aggravation. But not a disappointment, I assure you." He ran his eyes over her in a cool, contemplative appraisal that to her horrified consternation made her feel as if he'd just peeled off all her clothes. It also made her feel hot, uncomfortable, and disturbingly conscious of the faint male odor of his lean, undeniably attractive male body.

"I have to go," she said abruptly. "Michael will be waiting to see you."

"Michael has seen me twice a day since he landed himself in here. He'll manage very well without me for an hour or two. You and I are going down to the cafeteria to talk."

"But I have to go to Emergency," objected Bronwen, pulling away as he coiled his long fingers around her arm.

"Go later."

"No, I——"

She saw his lips tighten. "Bronwen Evans, my patience is wearing a little thin. I have had one helluva day at work, and when I got a chance to pick up the paper I discovered that my friend's sister had just managed to get herself killed. Then I find she's still very much alive, but with a tongue in her head that's recently been pickled in vinegar——"

"Yes, but I do have to visit Emergency," Bronwen interrupted. She didn't like the turn of this conversation.

"My dear, what you have to do is come down to the cafeteria with me, have a cup of coffee, and talk. And if you give me any more objections, I promise you, you will *be* an emergency. Do you understand?"

When he put it like that Bronwen understood very well. Besides, there was no urgency about getting the muddle straightened out. Whatever the paper said, she definitely hadn't sprouted wings and a halo. Or a tail, she thought, eyeing his tight-lipped face.

In any case, when Slade, grim-faced, took her firmly by the arm and marched her over to the elevator, she was disconcerted to find that she felt most tinglingly earthbound.

When he sensed her stiffen Slade glanced down at the top of her head. It was still pure carrot, he reflected. No one had, or ever would, refer to Bronwen's hair as auburn. He liked it, though. Always had. She wore it in the same simple style, hanging loose and straight until it thickened and belled out over her shoulders. The soft bangs were still there too—and the freckles, and the big gray eyes. She had a sweet face. Not beautiful, but soft, and innocent somehow. It was too bad that in the years since he had last seen her her disposition appeared to have taken a turn for the worse. It no longer matched her gentle features. He drummed his fingers absently against his thigh. He would have to do something about Bronwen. Convince her that bad temper didn't pay. On the whole, he looked forward to the prospect.

As they entered the noisy cafeteria he asked abruptly, "Had Michael seen the papers before you reached him?"

"No. I got there first."

"Good. At least he was spared that shock." He directed her to a relatively private table in the corner.

"Which you weren't," she taunted him, suspecting that in Slade's case the shock had not been all that disturbing.

"Which I wasn't," he agreed equably. "On the other hand, I had the pleasure of seeing a ghost come to life. With her tongue in good working order."

Bronwen frowned. "Was it a pleasure?" She had meant to sound scornful, but somehow the question came out more like a plea for reassurance.

His white-toothed smile didn't altogether reach his eyes. "At the time, yes. Very definitely. As to whether it will remain so..." He shrugged. "I'm beginning to wonder."

She opened her mouth, but before she could say anything Slade was walking away.

"Wait here," he said over his shoulder. "Tea or coffee?"

"Tea, please," replied Bronwen, who preferred coffee, but knew he knew it, and felt a contrary urge to surprise him.

After he left it occurred to her that, as surprises went, and considering the shock she had already given him today, her preference in beverages wasn't likely to rate high on his list of riveting concerns.

She was right. When he came back he dumped a metal pot of tea in front of her with a tight smile, sat down, and demanded, "All right. Now tell me what that nonsense in the paper was all about."

Bronwen swallowed. "It wasn't my fault," she said, resenting his tone, yet a little daunted by the steel blue glint in his eye.

Slade shook his head. "Did you learn that line from your brother?"

Her resentment grew. Maybe that *was* one of Michael's favorite lines, but Slade had no business to criticize her brother. Not after the trouble he himself had caused. It might have happened eight years ago, but because of Michael's impulsive decision to follow him to Canada the repercussions of Slade's behavior had changed her life.

"I *am* capable of speaking for myself," she said, lifting her chin.

"Are you? You used not to be."

"Maybe I just didn't choose to speak to you." She stirred sugar into her cup and didn't look at him. It was easier not to, because in the years since she had last set eyes on him he had acquired an aura of strength and a mature masculinity that he hadn't possessed to such a powerful degree in his youth. And it was remarkably seductive. She had always been aware that his firm, almost cruel mouth, and the chiseled, aquiline features beneath the waving blond hair had a magnetism about them that hadn't been lost on the eager young ladies of Pontglas. But in those days she had been more or less immune. Now she wasn't so sure—and, if she had to fall for any man, she certainly didn't intend it to be Slade.

She lifted the cup to her lips, and saw that his long, tapered fingers were tapping rhythmically against the table. When she glanced up with a feeling that there was something a bit threatening about those fingers she found his eyes fixed on her like cold blue glass.

"No," he said. "You didn't choose to speak to me, did you? As I remember, you were too busy making sheep's eyes at Lloyd Morgan."

Bronwen felt a flush starting at her neck, and rising up to cover her ears. "Lloyd?" she mumbled, unable to look away from that cold gaze. "I—I wasn't—Lloyd wasn't . . ."

"No, he most certainly wasn't," agreed Slade.

She closed her eyes, knowing the flush was making her look like an overcooked carrot. Memories of the past came flooding back. So even Slade had known about her infatuation for Lloyd. Yes, of course he had. The whole village had known. And if he had tried deliberately to hurt her, as perhaps he had, he couldn't have said anything more calculated to make her feel like a silly, naive little schoolgirl. She still couldn't think of Lloyd without reliving those days when she had wanted to hide in the most secluded corner she could find so that no one could ever laugh at her again.

Through a haze of embarrassment she heard Slade's voice saying firmly, "Now, then, Bronwen, as far as I'm concerned, red hair is no excuse for bad temper. And I want to know how that article got in the paper."

That Bronwen could cope with. "So do I," she said woodenly as her skin returned to its normal freckled pallor.

"You mean you don't know?"

"And how should I know? I came straight to the hospital from the airport. After I'd seen Michael I got a taxi. I meant to ask the driver to take me to an inexpensive hotel. But we were hit by a car, and I found myself back in the hospital in no time."

"Were you hurt?" he asked sharply.

"No, no. Just a few bruises, and a bit of a cut on my neck. My hair hides it. They let me go right away." When she saw that he looked unexpectedly grim she added dryly, "I wasn't pleased to find out I was dead either, so you can stop staring at me as if you wish that story were true."

Slade slammed his cup onto the table so forcefully that Bronwen expected it to crack. "I do not—yet—bear you any ill will, Bronwen Evans. I do, though, wish that this place were a little less public."

"Why?" she asked doubtfully.

"Push me too far and you may find out."

"Huh," scoffed Bronwen. "If you're talking caveman stuff it doesn't impress me at all." It did in a way, though, because her traitorous mind immediately induced visions of firm male thighs, and Slade's hands touching her where they shouldn't . . .

When she glanced across at him she saw that he was smiling, a superior, disbelieving smile that convinced her he guessed exactly what she was thinking.

"Doesn't it?" he said. "But I'm not sure that I want to impress you."

"Well, that's just as well, because you don't," said Bronwen sourly.

"I see." His expression was as cool as his voice. "Would you care for a piece of pie, my dear? Bitter lemon perhaps?"

She looked at him more closely, and saw just the trace of a quiver pulling at the edge of his mouth. Good grief. The man was laughing at her. Or trying not to.

She supposed she ought to see the funny side herself. The two of them hadn't seen each other for eight years, and then he read that she'd been killed. When he discovered that the story wasn't true, and was still recovering from the shock, she had greeted him like a long-lost enemy. Only they hadn't really been enemies in the old days, she recollected. It was only after he'd left with Michael, and she'd found out what he'd done, that her dislike of him had become so acute. No wonder he was exasperated by her attitude. Not, she thought glumly, that he showed any signs of letting it get him down. And he could laugh if he liked, but she *couldn't* forgive him for the past. He had hurt too many innocent people.

"No," she said now, refusing to let herself give him even the ghost of a smile. "I wouldn't like any pie, thank you. What I would like is to know how Michael got into this mess. He wouldn't tell me." She didn't like Slade, but if he insisted on keeping her company she might as well find out what she could.

"I'm not surprised," he answered her.

Bronwen frowned. "Why? Michael's not a fighter."
She paused. "Oh. I suppose you mean *you*..."

"No, Miss Vinegar Tongue, I do not mean me. I'm
not in the habit of engaging in street brawls. Unless
I'm pushed."

"Oh. Then you mean Michael——"

"I'm really not sure what I mean, as I wasn't there.
However, I do have ways of getting information. It
appears that your brother was coming out of a pub
with a group of friends, when his eye lighted on—"
he hesitated, choosing his words "—on a particularly
curvaceous young lady with a rather obvious symbol
coyly tattooed across her cheek. Michael must have
taken it as an invitation."

"And it wasn't?"

Slade's smile was austere. "Oh, it was. But not for
him, as he might have known. He found that out when
her boyfriend emerged from a doorway, along with
an armed support group. I gather a sordid little fracas
ensued, at the end of which the police arrived,
knocked a few heads together, arrested Michael's attacker, who was in the process of wiping blood off
his knife—and your brother ended up here on a
stretcher."

"Oh, dear." Bronwen was horrified. "Things like
that don't happen in Pontglas." She paused. "Well,
except that one time when Mrs. Jones chased Mrs.
Griffiths down the high street with a potato peeler
because Mrs. Griffiths called Mr. Jones a randy old
goat. Which he was."

"Mmm." Slade stretched his legs and smoothed a
hand over his mouth. "I remember. The situations
have certain similarities, I agree."

Their eyes met with a hint of wary amusement, and
for a moment they shared a memory of the past that

made Bronwen feel a surprising intimacy with this man who, a few seconds earlier, had been driving her to thoughts of calculated assault.

"You said you weren't with Michael," she said carefully, pushing aside all thoughts of intimacy and trying not to think about the gray-clad knee that had, very briefly, brushed up against her own.

"No. You'll be relieved to know that I've been trying to keep out of Michael's life as much as possible lately." He paused, and then went on with a crispness that might have masked regret, "At one time we used to travel all over the country together, as I suppose he told you. But after we moved down here I decided it was time to put down roots. Naturally, when Michael asked for a job with the company I was in the process of forming I was glad to oblige him."

Bronwen eyed him skeptically. "You were?"

"Don't look so surprised. Whatever you may imagine, letting down my friends has never been one of my vices, and I've always thought your feckless brother had hidden strengths if only he'd give himself a chance. I suppose that's why we lasted together so long. But I'm afraid Michael wasn't willing to put in the hours I expected of him, so he quit. Got himself his own place, and his own friends, along with a job in a bar. He told me he could manage without me. In a way, I was relieved to hear it."

"And could he? Manage?"

Slade shrugged, and her eyes widened as she watched the muscles pull tight beneath his shirt. "If getting oneself stabbed is 'managing' then I suppose the answer has to be yes."

Bronwen glared at him. "In other words, true to form, you *did* let him down."

Slade's eyes hardened. "True to form?"

"Well, it's not the first time, is it? You let someone else down once. Very badly."

"What are you getting at, Bronwen?" His hands curled around his cup and he leaned across the table as if he would prefer them to be curled around her. And not with any kind of affection.

Bronwen frowned. He was giving an impressive performance as a man who was genuinely mystified and more than a little angry. Her opinion of him sank a step lower. Didn't he even have the decency to admit his guilt?

"I think you know what I'm getting at," she replied, turning her head to stare with feigned fascination at a handsome young intern who was setting his tray down on the next table.

"Not being a mind reader, I know nothing of the sort," he snapped. "Perhaps you'll enlighten me."

He *was* genuinely angry. There was no doubt about it. Well, she certainly had to give him marks for gall. Apparently he thought he had a right to treat people any way he chose, with no sort of accountability.

"I don't believe there's any need for explanations," said Bronwen, pouring the remainder of her tea into her cup. Her hand wasn't quite steady, and some of the liquid splashed onto the table.

"Distracted by the view?" Slade taunted, with a meaningful glance at the intern.

Bronwen chose not to reply.

Slade stared at her, his features blank. "Very well," he said finally. "I can't force you to answer me. At least not here."

She didn't like the sound of that. "No," she said. "You can't. Especially when you already know the answer. To get back to Michael——"

"I'm not interested in getting back to Michael."

"Well, I am. He's my brother."

"He is also twenty-nine years old, and capable of making his own decisions."

Yes, she supposed that was true in a way. Michael's decisions weren't always the right ones, and often they were governed more by impulse than by common sense—a prize example being his sudden whim to accompany Slade to Canada without stopping to think that his old-fashioned parents had counted on handing over the family business to their son. To them, a daughter, although they loved her deeply, was not the same. She had resented that for a long time, she remembered with a certain sadness. But in the end it had made her more determined to be independent, to prove to them, and to herself, that she could succeed as well as any boy.

And she had. The shop had made a slightly higher profit in the years since she had taken it over.

None of which altered the fact that she was sitting across from a man who, for all her independence, could still intimidate her merely by narrowing an eye. He was narrowing both eyes now.

"If you can stop mentally devouring that pink-cheeked youth at the next table," said Slade, "perhaps we should be moving on. We still have a fair amount to do this afternoon."

Bronwen stopped feeling intimidated and felt murderous. "I am not devouring anybody," she muttered. It had to be a mutter, or the pink-cheeked youth would have heard her. "Except you, perhaps. And I don't mean that as a compliment."

"I wonder why that doesn't surprise me."

Bronwen felt as if her spine would snap if she sat up any straighter. "Is that all you have to say?" she demanded, making an effort to keep her voice low.

Somebody dropped a tray with a loud crash, and Slade let his chair down abruptly and stood up. "No. It's not. But, as I don't propose to say it here, for the present we'll head for Emergency to show them the corpus delecti. After which I will get you decently settled——"

"I'm already settled."

"Keep it up, and you may be. As I was saying, I'll get you settled. After that I'll buy you dinner—and we'll talk some more. At which point you're likely to find out that I have a lot more to say than you bargained on." He removed the cup that was clasped between her fingers, seized her hand and hauled her on to her feet. "Where's your luggage?" he demanded.

She told him.

"Good heavens. Surely even you can't be that stupid?"

"What do you mean?" she asked sweetly, contriving to grind her heel hard into his black-shod foot.

He swore. "I mean, that's the worst part of town you could have picked." His highly polished shoe descended deliberately across her instep.

"It's cheap," she gasped. The pressure was pinning her to the floor and, although it didn't hurt, she couldn't move.

Slade smiled grimly, and waited till her eyes dropped before he lifted his foot. "I don't care if they *pay* you to take their rooms. You're not staying there."

"I already am."

"Not any more you're not."

"Oh? And where do you suggest I move to?"

"I don't suggest." He caught her by the shoulder and propelled her at an undignified run toward the exit. "I'm moving you into my place. Within the hour." When he saw her lips part indignantly he added, "And if you give me any more arguments, I promise you, I'm not averse to that caveman stuff you mentioned. In fact, in my present frame of mind, I'm not sure it wouldn't do both of us a world of good."

CHAPTER TWO

BRONWEN maintained a haughty silence until they reached the street. Then she said icily, ignoring Slade's hand on her shoulder, "I suppose it's too much to ask where we're going?"

"Not at all. We're going across the road. To my car."

"I see." Her voice dripped honeyed sarcasm. "But, as the emergency department happens to be directly behind us, that hardly seems sensible, does it?"

Slade drew to an abrupt halt, and for the second time in the space of a few minutes Bronwen was treated to a demonstration of his proficiency in the more imaginative aspects of the English language. Then, without a word, he wheeled around and marched her back into the hospital.

She stole a glance at his face and tried to suppress a chuckle. He looked like a one-man storm cloud gathering over the Arctic. Served him right for being so bossy, she thought.

It took over an hour to sort out what Bronwen called "This ridiculous muddle," and what Slade muttered under his breath was "A lot of bloody incompetence."

The emergency department was suitably flabbergasted to discover that their deceased patient was alive and protesting her fate. But they weren't pleased, and she and Slade were promptly directed to Administration.

"They're responsible for admissions and discharges," explained a harried-looking young man who kept eyeing Bronwen as though he thought she might grow fangs and exhibit a disturbing interest in his neck.

"Dead or alive, presumably," murmured Slade.

At first, the formidable lady dragon whose job it was to sort out the confusion refused to believe Bronwen's story.

"Impossible," she snorted, waving them to seats in front of her desk. "Our staff are very careful with their record-keeping."

"I'm sure they are," said Bronwen soothingly. "Perhaps the mistake arose elsewhere. All the same, that report in the paper isn't true."

"Hmm." The dragon peered over her glasses, rose majestically to her feet, glared at them, and then strode away to conduct a whispered conversation with a colleague.

"She's very cross with me," remarked Bronwen with a mischievous glance at her companion's stony face. "I think she'd much rather I hadn't been resurrected."

"She's not convinced you are," said Slade dryly. He stopped looking stony, put his head on one side, and added pensively, "Come to think of it, you do look a bit white. Are you sure——?"

"Quite sure," said Bronwen, who once again was trying not to laugh. If Slade thought he'd get around her with that kind of poker-faced teasing he was wrong.

The dragon came back, and, after a good deal of paper-shuffling, throat-clearing and glaring, admitted that Bronwen Evans was apparently still alive. Barbara Evans, aged seventy-two, was not. Both of them had been involved in taxi accidents, and both of them were visitors from Britain. How the wrong Evans had ended up as an accident report in the paper was still a mystery. But it definitely wasn't the hospital's fault, they were assured with a lot more defensive glaring.

"Then whose fault is it?" demanded Slade, impaling the dragon with a forbidding blue eye.

"It doesn't matter," said Bronwen hastily. "I don't really care whose fault it is, and I don't care why I'm alive either. I just want it officially recorded that I am."

On top of everything else, she didn't think she was up to refereeing a battle of wills between a tight-lipped Slade and this guardian of the hospital's reputation.

"It has been so recorded," intoned the dragon in a sepulchral voice.

Bronwen nodded, rose quickly, and touched Slade's shoulder. "Can we go now, please?" she asked with a deliberate attempt to sound pathetic. "I'm very tired . . ."

Slade stood up. "All right. If that's all it takes to satisfy you——"

"Oh, yes, I'm quite satisfied." She noted his reluctance and grabbed his arm, clinging to it as if she needed support.

Slade stared down at her with a slight frown, then put his hand over hers.

In a very short time they were on the street.

Bronwen realized she was beginning to feel enormously hungry, and remembered that Slade had mentioned dinner. Unfortunately she also remembered that it was her intention to escape his clutches the moment the opportunity arose.

"I'm not staying with you," she said flatly, stepping away from him as they stood on the pavement, breathing in the warm May air. "And you needn't think your threats frighten me at all, because they don't."

Slade didn't answer.

"I said, I'm not staying with you," she repeated as he took her arm.

He still didn't answer, but his grip tightened and he urged her ahead of him across the road.

"Slade..." She knew there was a pleading note in her voice now, but she couldn't control it. "Slade, answer me."

"I thought you were tired." He pulled open the door of a bright red car and gestured at her to get in.

"And what has that to do with anything?"

"Just the fact that you don't sound a bit tired to me. You're too damn argumentative. Go on, get in."

She drew back, eyeing the red door doubtfully. Even though she knew nothing about cars, she had an idea this one might possibly be a Porsche.

"I am *not* going with you," she informed him, with as much conviction as she could muster.

"Oh, yes, you are. Get in."

She heard the implacable note in his voice, remembered how awful the hotel was, and how hungry she was. It would be so much easier to give in—nice to be taken care of—just for tonight.

If only he weren't Slade...

But he was Slade. Which, she thought later, was probably how it came about that in the space of less than five seconds she found herself being lifted off her feet and deposited briskly in the passenger seat of his car.

"And don't try it," he warned, swinging himself down beside her.

Her fingers, which had been moving surreptitiously toward the handle, stilled abruptly. As Slade leaned across and snapped her seat belt into place, once again she was conscious of the warm, enticing scent of him. When he put his foot on the accelerator her eyes were drawn to the taut curve of his thighs... She discovered she felt strangely lethargic.

She *didn't* try it, and in a moment the car was purring smoothly down the street.

"Good Lord," Slade muttered a little while later, after they had circled her hotel four times in search of a parking space, and eventually pulled up a block from their destination.

"What's the matter?" asked Bronwen. She resented the necessity of talking to him, but she was curious, wondering if he'd discovered a flat tire or some other, more serious problem.

"This slum. You must have gone out of your way to find sleazy." He opened her door, helped her out, and gestured at overflowing garbage cans, and a drunk snoring quietly in a doorway.

"No," she said shortly. "I told you, I went out of my way to find cheap. The whole world isn't as affluent as you are, Slade. People don't often live in places like this from choice."

"Ah," said Slade. "A reformer. Very commendable. What makes you think I'm affluent, by the way?"

Bronwen successfully conquered an urge to punch him on his supercilious nose. "I might have lived most of my life in a small village," she replied tartly, "but that doesn't mean I don't know a silk shirt when I see one. And, if I'm not very much mistaken, the flashy red batmobile that brought us here is a genuine, real live Porsche."

"You don't like my car?" he asked mildly.

"It's very nice," said Bronwen in a voice that oozed patronizing tolerance.

Slade's lips quirked. "A suitable toy for an overgrown little boy. Is that what you mean?"

Bronwen stole a quick look at him as he strode beside her so swiftly that she had to skip to keep up. She took in the strong profile, the straight shoulders and the air of being totally at ease in surroundings more suited to public transport than Porsches. No, definitely not a little boy.

"No," she said slowly. "The car suits you."

Slade made a face. "That almost sounds like a compliment. But, given your track record in that line, I suppose I should beware of complacence."

Bronwen tried not to smile. When he talked like that, and looked at her, all teasing and amused, it was perfectly possible to like Slade—until she remembered what he'd done.

"I think you were always a bit complacent," she said coolly, not allowing herself to take liking any further. "You had good reason to be, as far as that goes. Every girl in the village fell in love with you the moment you arrived to live with your aunt and uncle. And the boys admired you as well—even though they envied your popularity."

They came to a halt before the scratched brown door of her hotel, and Slade's eyes darkened. "There wasn't much to envy," he said curtly. "I was fifteen, trying desperately to appear a man of the world among people who'd known each other all their lives. The truth was that I was just a lonely kid whose parents had died in a house fire caused by a drunken father who fell asleep with a lighted cigarette. No great cause for complacence."

"Oh," said Bronwen uncomfortably. She'd heard Slade's history, of course—how he'd come home from a movie to find his less than ideal parents dead—but she had never heard him talk about it before. She glanced at his face, wondering if he was looking for sympathy, and at once saw that he wasn't. He was testing her, she decided, watching to see how she'd react, and wanting to put her off-balance, probably, so that she wouldn't resist him when he tried to browbeat her into moving into his apartment.

"You succeeded," she said succinctly.

"Succeeded?" He looked startled.

"Mmm. Most of us thought you were terribly sophisticated and exciting. Definitely a man of the world."

"Most of us?" he said softly, pausing outside the door of room six. "But not Bronwen Evans, of course." He touched the back of his hand to her cheek.

She laughed uneasily. "I thought you were flamboyant and very handsome," she said, not looking at him.

"Which didn't impress you."

"Not at all." She took a deep breath. "Slade, what are we doing here? Why don't you just go away, and leave me to——?"

"We're moving you out of this flea pit, that's what we're doing. And I've no intention of leaving you on your own in a strange city where you don't know a soul——"

"I know Michael."

"Who is flat on his back in the hospital, which is where he richly deserves to be. Unfortunately that doesn't help you."

"Slade, for heaven's sake, *listen*. I don't need help. I *can't* move in with you. It's not right."

"Why not? Afraid I'll take advantage of your charmingly convenient body?" The words were spoken flippantly enough, but Bronwen had a sense that he was angry.

"The thought had crossed my mind," she said dryly, wishing she could think of a more satisfactorily deflating response.

"Well, cross it out again. I'm not in the habit of seducing my friends' sisters. They seem not to like it, for some reason. On the other hand, if the sisters decide to seduce me . . ." His voice trailed off, and the blue eyes gleamed an unmistakable challenge.

"Unlikely." Tightening her lips, Bronwen put her key in the lock and pushed open the ill-fitting door. It squeaked loudly. If Slade thought she was going to rise to that sort of challenge he was deluding himself.

"I was afraid you'd say that," he murmured, stooping his wide shoulders to enter the sparsely furnished room. When he straightened again he blinked, and added incredulously, "Good grief. Bronwen, do you mean to tell me you actually managed to sleep in this floral nightmare? It looks like the result of some deranged researcher's efforts to produce cannibalistic sunflowers."

Bronwen giggled, her irritation momentarily forgotten. "I know. It's awful, isn't it?"

"An understatement. It also clashes with your hair. So, as we've definitely established that I'm not about to ravish you without consent, can we please collect your suitcases and get out of here before these damn flowers attack us? I have a feeling that one in the corner thinks I'm dinner."

"Don't be ridiculous." Bronwen thought of protesting again, but somehow this mocking, light-hearted Slade was much more persuasive than the domineering tyrant who had forced her to bring him here in the first place. This Slade she could almost trust. In any case, she certainly trusted herself—and he was right about the sunflowers. The one above the rickety dressing table seemed to have its malevolent black eye fixed on her.

She tucked a pair of slippers and a sensible white nightgown into her suitcase and closed the lid.

Two minutes later, as Slade took the stairs three at a time she was trotting along in his wake while she tried to puzzle out how he had succeeded in getting her to do exactly as he wanted. It was a perplexing question, because after running the shop on her own for five years Bronwen had come to expect that most things would be done exactly as *she* wanted.

Perhaps, she decided, the whole thing could be put down to culture shock, weariness, and a feeling, based more on hope than anything else, that Slade was only bullying her because he didn't want her to come to any harm. It wasn't really that she was playing Trilby to his Svengali. And, if she was, it wasn't a role she intended to play for very long.

When they reached the car they found it was surrounded by half a dozen small and grubby urchins. Inside the circle a teenager with several days' growth of beard was systematically picking the lock.

Briefly Bronwen closed her eyes. Slade had said he wasn't in the habit of engaging in street brawls, but he didn't strike her as the sort of man who would stand back and allow his property to be vandalized.

To her surprise, instead of bellowing with rage and wading in with both fists flying, he strode purposefully toward the absorbed little group, moved two small shoulders aside quite gently, and said in a voice that was pleasantly level but with an underlying edge of iron, "I believe I'll use my key, if you don't mind, as this does happen to be my car. Perhaps I can give you a lift somewhere? To the police station, I imagine."

The younger acolytes snickered, and the teenager with the beard looked up as if he had been hit on the head by the moon. His face turned a muddy red. "Don't you try nothing, mister," he began to bluster.

"I wasn't about to. And I suggest you don't try anything either, or you may regret it. However, if you ever decide you'd like to earn an honest living, here's my card. I could have a job for someone who's useful with his hands. As you obviously are." He gestured at the door of the Porsche, which had just swung open.

The boy's face turned from dark red to pale pink, and he shook his head as if to dislodge an unexpected impediment in his ears.

"You crazy?" he demanded, dark eyes wary.

"Possibly. Now, if you would all move out of the way I believe it's time I took this lady home."

Six mouths fell open in gaping disbelief as Slade held out his hand to Bronwen and ushered her through the stunned little crowd. The seventh, and oldest, mouth closed with a snap—but its owner backed off with the rest.

When Bronwen glanced in the mirror as they pulled away she saw that the entire gang, along with the drunk who had been sleeping in the doorway, were staring after them as if they'd just had a visitation from space. As, in a way, they had, she thought bemusedly. She couldn't imagine that Slade normally parked his car in this part of town. He'd only done it today because of her.

"I think that young man was right," she said finally. "You are crazy."

"Thank you. It's kind of you to say so."

"No, really, Slade. I mean, I have to admit you handled the situation beautifully, but why on earth did you offer him a job? Why did you risk your car here, for that matter? I could have taken the bus."

"No doubt you could. Probably to some other unsuitable flophouse. With poppies on the walls this time maybe." His long fingers tightened on the wheel. "I don't mean to let that happen, Bronwen. And of course I knew my car couldn't last long in these parts, but, as I didn't intend to stay long either, that was hardly an issue."

Bronwen nodded. "All right, that makes sense. Offering him a job doesn't."

"Maybe not. But I've walked a few miles in his shoes. Aimless, frustrated, broke, with parents who were usually too damn drunk to care. If they hadn't died, and Aunt Nerys hadn't taken in her wayward sister's child, I might have turned into a full-fledged petty criminal myself."

She stared at him, saw the thin lines at the sides of his chiseled mouth—and after a while she shook her head emphatically. "No," she said. "You wouldn't. You're too strong inside yourself for that. Arrogant, of course. But very strong." When he didn't answer she added with a grim little smile, "But if you had taken to crime you'd have been good at it. Not petty."

Cool eyebrows arched above glittering blue eyes as Slade turned his head to throw her a look of derision. "I thought it was too good to be true."

"What do you mean?"

"You *almost* paid me a compliment. How fortunate that you caught yourself in time."

Bronwen glared. "Supercilious as well as arrogant," she snapped.

"Ah. Much better. I knew you wouldn't let me down."

She saw that his lips were parted in a long, very self-satisfied grin, so she turned her head away and relapsed into a frowning silence. It wasn't broken until they pulled into the underground parking garage of a tall apartment block on Point Gray Road.

"It's dark in here," she said involuntarily as Slade swung open the door.

"Mmm. It often is underground. That's why we have things called lights."

"Yes, but..." Bronwen gulped and shut up. He was right. The place was quite adequately lighted. It was just that she had hated dim, enclosed spaces ever since Michael had locked her in a cupboard as a joke and then forgotten about her. She had been trapped there for over an hour, and the experience had left her with a permanent fear of the dark. But that was no reason to behave like a jittery schoolgirl in front of Slade—who was watching her and smiling an odd little smile.

"Come on," he said. "The elevator's this way."

She was quite glad to have him take her arm as their footsteps echoed across the concrete. It was impossible to feel really nervous with his powerful figure walking beside her—and the occasional touch of his thigh against her hip was reassuring as well as alarmingly exciting.

"It's very elegant," said Bronwen, wide-eyed, as the carpeted brass-fitted elevator purred smoothly and endlessly upward.

"Do you think so?" He smiled, and she felt ridiculously young and unsophisticated.

But when they finally stopped, and Slade ushered her through a doorway into the lightest, most breathtakingly beautiful room she had ever seen, in spite of herself she couldn't hold back a gasp.

"Like it?" he inquired laconically.

"It's—I . . . It's incredible."

And indeed it was. One whole wall was a window onto a wide balcony facing out over a sparkling, peridot colored sea. Inside, the green of the ocean was reflected in the muted blues and greens of the furnishings. The ceiling was high, adding to the feeling of air and space, and there was no carpet on the floor, only big green-and-white tiles. The pictures on the walls were, she recognized, by artists who didn't come cheap.

"Incredible in what way?" asked Slade dryly. "I suppose you mean it's bare and cold, and totally unlike your cozy home?"

"Well, it's certainly unlike home," she admitted, thinking of the prints, chintzes and frilly lamp shades that she hadn't bothered to change since her parents' day. "But it's not bare. Uncluttered certainly. But I think it's right for the space."

"So you approve." He picked up a lock of her hair and tucked it behind her ear. "I'm glad."

Something in his tone made Bronwen glance at him sharply, but his lips were curled in a smooth little smile, and his eyes gave nothing away.

"Where are the bedrooms?" she blurted—and then could have kicked herself for asking.

The smooth smile turned into a leer, exactly as she had known it would. "Bedroom," he corrected her. "There's only one."

Bronwen felt the flush starting at her neck and moving upward, and she turned away from him quickly.

Behind her Slade laughed softly. "I'm not Blue-beard," he assured her.

"Aren't you? That's debatable. But..."

"But you hadn't planned to share my bed? Don't worry, I may survive the shattering disappointment."

Oh, you'll survive it all right, thought Bronwen sourly. Because you're not shattered one bit. You're laughing at me.

Aloud, all she said was, "That's the second great relief I've had today. May I ask just where you *do* expect me to sleep?"

"In my bedroom."

That did it. She had suffered a temporary lapse of sanity, but now she'd recovered.

Long before she reached the door Slade caught up with her. "Don't run away," he said, taking her by the arm and spinning her firmly around. "I won't let you, you know."

"You can't stop me." She swallowed, noting the cynical glint in his eye. "At least——"

"At least I *can*, but you hope I won't," he finished for her, lifting his free hand and curling it around the back of her neck. "Sorry to dash your hopes, my dear, but I most certainly will stop you."

For the first time since she'd almost bumped into him in the hospital corridor Bronwen felt a little afraid of Slade. She'd been frustrated and irritated with him earlier. Intimidated even. But not afraid.

It must have shown in her eyes, because he released her abruptly, and said with a trace of impatience, "For goodness' sake, Bronwen, what do you think I am?

I'll sleep out here on the sofa. *You* will have the bedroom to yourself."

"Oh," she said, feeling foolish again. After all, she had come here of her own free will.

"Will that suit your ladyship," he asked caustically.

She wasn't sure it would suit her at all, but it was probably too late to change her mind. She needed a place to stay, she was fairly confident Slade wouldn't take advantage, and for one night at least it would be easier to go along with him than argue. Although his behavior eight years ago had been callous and reprehensible, no one had ever suggested he'd forced himself on an unwilling victim.

"It suits me," she replied primly.

"Good. I'm glad to have met with your approval. Finally." He ran a handkerchief in exaggerated relief across his forehead. "And, now that we have that settled, what would you like to do. Eat here, or go out to dinner before we visit your brother?"

Bronwen asked him doubtfully. "Do you mean you can cook?" she asked, surprised.

"Certainly not. But you can."

She gasped. "Well, of all the backhanded invitations I've ever had, that has to be the most self-serving ..."

"I usually do manage to serve myself, as you've pointed out. But you can wipe that look of outrage off your freckled face. Mrs. Doyle, my housekeeper, is on holiday, so she's left the freezer stocked with dishes which even I can manage to cope with."

"Oh," said Bronwen.

"'Oh'" isn't an answer."

"Answer?"

"Bronwen, I don't really think you're stupid. At least, you used not to be. Do you want to eat in or out?"

What she actually wanted to do was hit him. She started to say "Oh" again, then bit it back. "In," she said. "It'll be easier."

It probably wouldn't be easier, but she was reluctant to let Slade pay for her meal, and she had a feeling he would flatly refuse to allow her to buy her own. Another argument was the last thing she was in the mood for tonight.

"Right," he said, bending down to pick up her suitcases. "In that case, I'll show you your room."

Once again Bronwen found herself trotting behind Slade, as he led the way through a blue-painted doorway to a small bedroom decorated in brown and gold. It was warm, intimate, a surprising contrast to the airiness of the rest of the suite.

"Oh!" she exclaimed. "It has the same clean lines as the other part, but it's different..."

"Mmm," agreed Slade. "I like to be warm in bed." The oblique glance he threw at her would have made her blush if she had allowed herself to meet his eyes. It was a very big bed, she noted, made of dark wood, with a golden yellow cover...more than enough room for two people...

She sat on the thought quickly.

"Did you decorate this place yourself?" she asked, more to take her mind off the bed and the activity that must have gone on there than because she really wanted to know.

"I did not. That's why I have people to work for me. I told them what I wanted done, and they did it."

Bronwen frowned, and began to unlock the cases he had tossed on the bed. "Work for you?" she repeated. "What, actually, do you do, Slade?"

He sighed. "Don't look at me as though you suspect me of white slavery. The truth is much less exciting."

"What is the truth, then?"

"Just that after years of traveling around the country from job to job, and spending a whole lot of time in trailers and mobile homes, I got a feel for the motor-home business. So I decided to design and market my own."

"What with?" asked Bronwen, who always saw the practical side of things. "That takes capital."

"I managed to get backers," he said, sounding surprised—as indeed he probably was, she realized half resentfully. Slade had always expected to get what he wanted, and had rarely admitted the possibility of failure.

"And you were successful in your enterprise, of course," she said with a small, dry smile.

"You might say so."

Yes, she thought, taking in the room with its quietly luxurious appointments, remembering the Porsche and the silk shirt. Yes, she certainly might say so. Not bad for a kid who had grown up on the wrong side of the tracks, and then moved to a small country village. Not bad at all.

"Food," said Slade, taking her arm and causing her to jump. "You can leave the unpacking till later."

He put his arm casually around her waist and drew her back into the main room. When he released her the moment they reached the kitchen alcove she felt a startling, and thoroughly unwanted, sense of regret—which faded immediately when Slade said, "Right. There's the freezer," and waited for her to make the next move.

"Very nice," said Bronwen, gazing studiously out over the water.

"It has food in it."

"I'm delighted to hear it."

Beside her she heard a sigh of exasperation. "If you open the lid, my dear, you'll be able to find us something to eat."

"I thought you said that even *you* could manage to heat up already prepared dishes." She followed the passage of a boat with red sails as it drifted dreamily across the inlet.

"I might have said something of the sort in a weak moment, but I'm really very bad at cooking. You wouldn't want me to burn your dinner, would you?"

She looked at him then, and saw that he was rocking back on his heels with his hands in his pockets, wearing a disarming but very determined smile.

Lord, he's attractive, she thought instinctively. How strange that I never succumbed to his charms before. Not that she was succumbing now, she reminded herself hastily. On the other hand, she probably *was* cooking dinner. She enjoyed cooking, and she was good at it. Slade obviously wasn't, or was just too lazy and/or obstinate to try. On the whole, it might be a great deal easier on her digestion to give in. And he *was* offering her free room and board. Well, not offering exactly. Forcing it on her was more like it.

"All right," she said, shrugging indifferently so he wouldn't get the idea he had won any sort of major victory. "I'll fix supper. Where are the vegetables?"

"Vegetables?" he asked blankly. "Don't think I have any. Oh, maybe... Yes, now that I think of it, I believe I did see a bag of green slime lurking somewhere at the back of the fridge. On Tuesday. Or was it Monday?"

Bronwen rolled her eyes at the ceiling. Apparently cooking this meal was going to prove a much greater challenge than she'd expected.

The bag of green slime turned out to be an ancient and very liquid green pepper. It ended up in the garbage. Behind it she discovered a brown blob that might once have been lettuce. A package of carrots, however, seemed to have fared rather better. She set to work to peel them, while Slade wandered off, looking smug, and murmuring something about wine.

Later, after Bronwen had cooked up one of Mrs. Doyle's neatly marked casseroles, the two of them sat down at the polished pine table that separated the main living area from the kitchen.

At first they didn't speak at all. Bronwen because she felt on edge, unsure of herself, and Slade because he was aware that his guest was uncomfortable and wanted to see how long it would take her to break the silence.

It took almost five minutes. After a chunk of macaroni had wedged itself between her teeth, and Slade had watched with interest while she dislodged it, she finally could stand it no longer.

"Slade," she burst out, because food was on her mind and she had to say something or scream. "Slade, if you're such a terrible cook, how did you survive all those years when you were traveling around the country with Michael? It's obvious enough you didn't starve."

He smiled thinly. "Thank you. It's nice to know you don't think I'm undernourished."

Undernourished! Bronwen stared at him. No, he didn't look undernourished. With his spare figure and flat stomach, he was an almost perfect specimen of man. But she wasn't going to tell him that. "I asked how you managed to feed yourselves," she repeated coldly.

Slade put down his fork. "Your brother isn't a bad cook when he puts his mind to it," he said off-handedly. "Sometimes he did the cooking. Other times we worked in lumber camps or on construction projects where meals were provided for us. Does that answer your question?"

"I suppose so," said Bronwen.

"Good. Not that you give a damn, do you?"

"Not really," she agreed, hoping to even the score.

Slade's lips stretched in a malicious grin. "I thought not. In that case, you'll be sorry to hear that, when pushed, I'm even capable of fending for myself."

"I see," said Bronwen frigidly. "So that business about being a helpless male was just an act to—to get me to do all the work."

He shrugged. "I've never had the option of being helpless, Bronwen. But I do dislike cooking."

"And you very much *like* getting your own way. I might have known."

"You might," he agreed. "But apparently you didn't. This is very good, by the way."

Bronwen put her wineglass down quietly, before she was tempted to throw its contents in his face. "It should be. I'm sure you only employ the best."

"Now why do I get the idea that that comment wasn't meant to flatter me?" He closed one eye and held his glass to the light.

"Probably because it wasn't," said Bronwen shortly.

Slade put the glass down. "All right, Bronwen," he snapped, abandoning his air of detachment with alarming abruptness. "Let's put an end to this non-sense. I'm getting a bit tired of being treated as a combination of Caligula and the Pied Piper in modern dress. To the best of my knowledge I have never done you an injury——''

''You haven't,'' Bronwen assured him. ''I'm not the issue.''

She watched the slight flaring of his nostrils, noted the hard set of his mouth and the narrowed eyes—and to her disgust she found herself suppressing a shiver.

''And *what*, may I ask, *is* the issue?'' His voice was low, dangerous, and Bronwen clutched her napkin tightly in her lap. But she had started this, and she wasn't going to be the one to back down.

''Jenny Price,'' she said evenly, knowing her face had turned red and that her eyes were probably much too bright.

''Jenny Price?'' Now Slade reminded her of an eagle poised to fall on its prey. ''What has Jenny Price got to do with *you*? Or me, for that matter?''

Bronwen couldn't believe what she was hearing. ''How can you ask that?'' she demanded, her voice rising in spite of her effort to keep calm.

''It strikes me as a perfectly reasonable question. You refuse to trust me, you shrink away from me as if I'm some sort of monster, and, when I ask you why, you say, 'Jenny Price.'''

Bronwen swallowed. ''All right,'' she said, her voice extra cold and distinct. ''If you want it spelled out for you, perhaps it hasn't escaped your memory that you got Jenny pregnant when she was already engaged to Brice Barker. Or that when she broke down and told him, and he threatened to kill you, you skedaddled out of town so fast that we could scarcely see the tail between your legs. So, no, I don't trust you. There isn't a reason on earth why I should. And if I shrink away from you it's because—because I don't want to end up like poor Jenny.''

CHAPTER THREE

BRONWEN wasn't looking at Slade. She was staring at her empty plate, and remembering how the news had burst upon the village that the glamorous Slade had fled from Brice Barker's wrath. Later the phone call had come from Michael.

By that time both young men were in London, and her brother had announced with the thoughtless cruelty of youth that they wouldn't be coming back to Pontglas.

"But where are you going to live?" her mother's soft voice had wailed.

Bronwen still remembered the look on that gentle woman's face when Michael had answered, "Canada." She remembered Jenny's face, too, as it had looked for many months after. Sad, frightened, with desolation deep in her eyes.

Gradually Bronwen's mind returned to the present, as she became aware that Slade was speaking, and that the cutting edge of his voice was slicing through her memories like a knife.

"Where did you hear that fascinating little tale?" he was asking coldly. "And what makes you think you're in danger of ending up like Jenny?"

She looked up then. His face was as closed and cold as a death mask, except that his skin wasn't actually white. It was very pale, though—the paleness of an anger he was having trouble keeping under control.

"I—I heard it from—I don't know who I heard it from," she admitted, twisting the edge of her napkin beneath the table. "The whole village was talking about it after you left. Brice never said a word to a soul, and if anyone asked him he offered to punch out their teeth for them. But the word got around anyway. I think someone must have heard part of a private conversation, and Brice didn't contradict the story. Nor did Jenny. He married her in the end, though, and gave the baby his name." She smoothed the napkin over her knees. "I think they were even happy in a quiet way—until Brice was killed in a mining accident two years ago."

"I see." Slade's face didn't change. "The baby— *my* baby," he added bleakly. "What is it? A boy or a girl?"

Bronwen's eyes opened very wide, and she didn't bother to hide her disgust. "Didn't you care enough to find out?" she asked him. "Bobby isn't a baby any more, Slade. He's a little boy. He'll be eight years old in a few months."

"I see," said Slade again. He pushed himself back from the table, got up, and strode across to the window. When he turned his back on her the sun made a burning halo of his hair. "So that's why..." He paused for a moment, and then began again. "All right, so now I know how you heard about my—shall we say, my indiscretion? But you haven't answered my other question. Why do you think you're in danger of ending up like Jenny?"

"I—I didn't mean that." Bronwen stole a glance at his profile, didn't like what she saw there, and busied herself with a leftover crusty roll.

"Really? How interesting. And by that do you mean you've decided I'm a reformed character? Or that you're not the sort of woman you imagine I fancy in bed?"

"I—*neither*," stuttered Bronwen, not knowing what she meant, except that she was certain he hadn't reformed, and she wished she were anywhere but alone with him in this room.

"Is that so?" Slade swung around to face her, his tall frame etched against the light, his face in shadow. He pressed his palms against the windowsill. "In that case, it has to be yourself you don't trust, doesn't it? It seems this is going to be my lucky night."

When Bronwen gasped he took a step toward her, and now she could see the malignant curve of his lips and the glitter of hard purpose in his eye.

"What are you doing?" she cried, gripping the edge of the table. "Slade, you can't..."

He stood still. "I can, you know," he said softly.

"No. You promised."

Slade laughed, and the sound made her shiver. "But surely," he said, "you don't expect the despoiler of poor little Jenny to keep a promise?"

Suddenly Bronwen found she wasn't distraught or confused any more. She was angry. How dared Slade speak of Jenny, whose life he had almost ruined, with that ugly sneer in his voice?

But there was no point taking him to task for it. He had shown all too clearly that he wasn't a man capable of remorse. However, there *was* some point in putting an end to this scene.

"Yes," she said. "Yes, Slade, I do expect you to keep your promise. In case you've forgotten, I happen to be Michael's sister."

"Ah, yes, Michael. No, I hadn't forgotten." He didn't sound cold and cruel any more. He sounded as if he had something lodged in his throat. "You love Michael, don't you?"

"Of course I do," she said impatiently. "He's my brother."

"Yes." He looked at his watch, and once more his face was in shadow. "Of course you do." Bronwen said nothing, and when he spoke again his voice was neutral, almost indifferent. "So we'd better be going if you want to visit the hospital again tonight. In the meantime, you and I have to come to an understanding."

"Understanding?"

"That's what I said. For one thing, as long as you're in Vancouver you'll be staying with me——"

"No! I can stay at Michael's place—once I get him to tell me where it is." She spoke quickly, hoping she didn't sound as panicked as she felt.

"You cannot stay at Michael's apartment. It's not suitable."

"Of course it is——"

"Don't argue with me. I didn't remove you from the frying pan just so you could walk into the fire. Take my word for it, Bronwen, Michael's apartment is *not* suitable."

Strangely, considering how she felt about Slade, and about his callous indifference to Jenny and his own child, Bronwen did take his word for it. There was something rocklike in his face that convinced her he was only telling the truth. Besides, it would be just like Michael to rent the kind of place he couldn't show to his sister.

"Very well," she said, with what she hoped was quiet dignity. "I suppose you should know. And what, then, is this understanding you're talking of?"

He ran a hand through his hair and said curtly, "I want you to stay here, Bronwen. But I *don't* propose to share my home with a carrot-haired shrew who misses no opportunity to let me know that she has a low opinion of my life-style, my morals, my character...in fact, everything about me, with the possible minor exception of my taste in interior decoration.''

Not just your taste in interior decoration, thought Bronwen as he hooked his thumbs into his belt and lounged across the room to stand beside her. No woman in her right mind could have a low opinion of that magnificent body. She stifled the thought instantly, though, when he put his hands on her upper arms and pulled her upright.

"Now," he said, leaning over her so that their noses were almost touching, "as I was saying, I'm not putting up with it, Bronwen. You can think what you like about me, it's a free country, but as long as you're here you'll refrain from throwing the past in my face, and behave with at least decent civility.''

"Don't you mean *servility*?" she interrupted him sweetly.

His fingers curled around her arms, but there was a weary note in his voice when he replied, "Don't push me too far, please. I'm fast losing patience."

"You terrify me," she scoffed. "And what would you do if I did?"

"Did what?"

"Push you too far?"

A dangerous light replaced the bleak look in his eyes. She didn't like it, especially when he replied much too gently, "You really want to know, don't you? All right, I'm becoming almost as anxious to show you. Come along.''

He released her arms, spun her around, put a firm hand on the small of her back and began to push her purposefully toward the sea green sofa.

"Hey," she gasped. "Slade, what do you think you're doing?"

"I thought you wanted to find out."

She pulled away from him and turned around, almost cannoning into his broad chest. "Oh, do stop this silly Neanderthal stuff," she snapped. "If you think I'd let you make love to me——"

"I don't. There are other ways of dealing with masculine frustration. Not to mention aggravating women."

Bronwen took a deep breath. "If you want to bring up aggravation I'd say you've got a monopoly on that."

"I doubt it." He cupped his hands around her cheeks. "Now, then, my carrot-haired fiend, I suggest we stop quarreling for the present, and come to some reasonable agreement."

It wasn't a bad idea, she supposed glumly, staring at the flat line of his mouth. For one thing, she didn't think she could take much more of this constant snapping and snarling. And, as Slade had said, it was a free country. She *could* think what she liked about him in private.

"What sort of agreement?" she asked warily.

He dropped his hands to his sides. "That I provide you with room and board. No strings attached, except that you refrain from sharpening your claws on me. I'm not a tree trunk, and I don't enjoy it. And no, I don't want servility, Miss Evans. A little common civility will do quite well." His lips curled in a confident smile, as if he knew he had the upper hand.

Bronwen eyed him sourly. It was true she hadn't been nice to him. She hadn't had much reason to be. He was bossy and overbearing, and eight years ago he had disrupted several people's lives. But today he

had been helpful, in his way. She couldn't deny that.
And he seemed to have some loyalty to Michael, who
must have been hard to put up with at times.

"Very well," she said finally. "You have my agreement."

When he only stared at her and didn't say anything
she held out her hand.

He took it. "That's a very dull way to seal a deal,"
he said softly. There was an odd look in his eyes now.
A sort of strain, almost as if something was causing
him pain.

"What do you mean?" she asked uncertainly.

"This." Before she could remove her hand he had
drawn her toward him, and was bending over her.
Then, very lightly, he brushed his lips over hers.

She gasped, surprised and stunned by the intensity
of her response to a kiss that was so short-lived that
it was hardly a kiss at all.

"Now, wasn't that better than a handshake?"
prompted Slade, his blue eyes very bright and pro-
voking.

"No. Yes—I ..." She turned away, not knowing
where to look, and eventually fixed her gaze on a small
watercolor of whitely churning waters breaking gently
over seaweed-covered rocks. "It's not to happen
again," she said woodenly.

"If you say so. Not that a great deal did happen,
did it? More's the pity."

She lifted her head. "Slade, if you're going to keep
that up——"

"I'm not. In future I promise to keep my hands
off you. Come on, it's time we left to see Michael."
He seized her hand.

"The dishes——"

"Forget the dishes."

Bronwen looked at the square white clock on the wall. They would *have* to forget them, although it went very much against her grain. She couldn't remember ever having walked out on a sinkful of unwashed dishes. Another example of Slade's deplorable influence on her hitherto exemplary behavior.

She sighed, pulled her hand away, and went to powder her freckles.

When they reached the hospital they found that Michael, presumably worn out after a day of serious flirtation, was almost asleep. They stayed just long enough to wish him well, and left with a promise to return the next day.

"I don't think you need to worry over much about that one," remarked Slade as they rode back down in the elevator. "He'll be up and about in no time."

"Yes," agreed Bronwen with a sigh. "And no doubt making eyes at every pretty girl who comes near him. I do wish he'd find a proper girlfriend and settle down."

"Mmm. He's twenty-nine. A year younger than I am," Slade mused. "Do you think perhaps I ought to settle down too? With a very *proper* young lady?"

Bronwen ignored the provocative gleam in his eye. "You're not my responsibility," she said primly. When he didn't answer she couldn't resist adding, "But any woman who could keep *you* in order would have my undying admiration."

The elevator thumped to a stop. "Would she, now?" he murmured, taking her elbow. "You think I need keeping in order, do you?"

"Very much so, but I'm afraid the task is impossible." She tossed her head, and her hair brushed his shoulder as they stepped out into the twilight.

Slade looked down at her with an expression that would have surprised her had she seen it. "Oh, I wouldn't be too sure of that," he drawled. "You never know. I might be putty in the hands of the right woman."

"You'd be in her hands, all right," agreed Bronwen. "I don't doubt that. But I'm certain you wouldn't be putty."

Beside her she heard the sound of a laugh being summarily stifled, and immediately she realized what she'd said. Thank the Lord the light was fading. At least Slade couldn't see the color of her cheeks. All the same, when she thought about it there was something very seductive about the idea of holding his firm body between her hands, running them across his chest and down his back...

They reached the car, and she slammed the door on her wayward thoughts. Slade was appallingly desirable. Even she, who wasn't in the habit of desiring, couldn't fail to appreciate that. He was also about as safe as a rattlesnake. As Jenny Price had found out to her cost.

But when Slade snapped on the light in his apartment half an hour later it wasn't rattlesnakes that came to mind. It was the fact that she was alone at the top of a very tall building with a man who was casually unbuttoning his shirt and tossing it at the nearest chair.

"What are you doing?" she gasped, trying to keep the panic from her voice, and her eyes from the enticing expanse of his chest.

"What does it look like?"

"It looks as if you're—undressing."

"Only partially. It's a warm night." His fingers moved to the buckle of his belt.

"Slade!" she exclaimed, giving up all pretense of sophistication. "You can't do that."

"Do what?"

"Take your pants off. It's—it's..."

"Conduct unbecoming a gentleman unless he has seduction in mind," he finished for her. "Don't worry. I rarely give in to temptation. And in this case I only wanted to see that wonderful expression of outrage in your big gray eyes. Which I did. It's made up for quite a few of the day's frustrations." He smiled with such complacent charm that Bronwen couldn't make up her mind whether she wanted to laugh, cry, or throw the nearest large blue cushion at his head.

In the end she just shook her head and sat down rather heavily on the sofa.

At once Slade lowered himself beside her and placed an arm carelessly along the back. She could feel his fingers touching her hair.

She glanced sideways, taking in the warm gold of his skin, breathing the faint odor of expensive aftershave and man. She swallowed, wondering if she would be able to handle what was left of this evening.

It was all very well to trust herself, and in a strange sort of way to trust Slade—but she'd had so little experience with men. Oh, she was twenty-six years old, and of course she'd been out with a few boys. But the shop had kept her busy, and since the fiasco of Lloyd Morgan she'd been vulnerable, and in no hurry to let her feelings run away with her heart.

She stared at the lights of the room reflected in the big window, and became conscious that Slade was toying with her hair. Lloyd. She mustn't forget Lloyd. It was too easy to forget that things were not always as they seemed. And sometimes they were exactly as they seemed ...

Beside her, Slade watched the small frown crease her forehead, saw her body sag a little, and wondered what this maddening, exasperating redhead was thinking up to torment him with next. It would help to know. He smiled speculatively, and dropped a hand over her shoulder.

Bronwen scarcely felt it. She was wondering how Jenny had felt when Slade had deserted her. And from Jenny her thoughts shifted to Lloyd. Lloyd, who had always been so nice to her, and over whom she had suffered such pangs of youthful heartache. But instead of becoming her steady boyfriend, as he always did in her dreams, he had left the village very suddenly with a black cloud of scandal over his head.

The most notable thing about the scandal was that it had involved not one, but three young women, and a large amount of money that was missing from his place of employment.

"What are you thinking?" asked Slade, quietly interrupting her thoughts.

She hesitated. But, after all, it was no great secret. The whole village had known about her infatuation. "I was thinking of Lloyd Morgan," she said.

"Good Lord." That was the last thing Slade had expected. "Don't tell me you still——?"

"No, no," she said quickly, turning to look at him at last. "It's just that sometimes I think it's a good thing—to remember."

"Why would you want to remember that? I know you had a childish crush on him, but the man was a rotten little thief who chased after everything in skirts. You must know that."

"You're a fine one to talk. And yes, of course I know. It's not that."

"What is it, then?"

Bronwen heard the note of impatience. "Just that—it's not a bad thing to keep in mind that it's very easy to get hurt when you give your heart too easily. Without thinking." There was a wealth of accusation in her words.

"And in your case without the faintest understanding of the man to whom you were giving it," said Slade grimly.

"I was young," she agreed, twisting a button on her sweater, which had suddenly become much too hot.

"And surprisingly innocent," he said, in a tone she hadn't heard him use before. "Unusual in this day and age."

"Of course it was unusual," said Bronwen, irritated by what she took for patronizing amusement. "That's why everyone laughed. They all knew Lloyd was a teenage Casanova."

"Not everyone laughed."

"No, that's true. My parents didn't. And you didn't," she added, her eyes opening wide as she remembered with some surprise that it was true. That was odd too. In those days Slade had laughed at almost everything.

"No," he replied. "I didn't think it was funny. Nor do I think you should spend the rest of your life avoiding any kind of relationship on the off chance that you might get hurt again."

"I'm not," said Bronwen indignantly. "It's just made me—cautious, that's all. Besides, I haven't had much time for what you call 'relationships.'" She gave him a quick, dry little smile. "It's also a fact that the selection of eligible men around Pontglas hasn't improved noticeably since you left. Rather the opposite."

"Hmm." Slade brushed a hand over his mouth. "I suppose it's too much to hope you meant that remark as anything other than an accurate, very boring statement of fact."

"Much too much," said Bronwen.

He laughed, and she recognized a moment too late that it was a predatory sort of laugh. She started to inch away, but his hands were already on her waist, and as she gaped up at him, stunned, he pulled her slowly into the circle of his arms. In the next instant her unresisting body was crushed against the hard surface of his chest.

"Wh—what...?" she mumbled into his neck. 'Slade——''

Her words were cut off as he moved his head to close his mouth over hers. And this was no feather-light kiss that left her wondering if it had really happened. It was purposeful, determined, the hunter taking rightful possession of his prey...

Except that this particular prey was a willing victim. She knew she ought to struggle—to push him away. But she couldn't. She had been kissed before, of course, but never like this. As if time had come to a standstill, and there was only this moment, here in Slade's arms, her whole body aflame with a desire that only he could put out.

When he released her, after completing the business he had started with a leisurely thoroughness that left her reeling, she fell back against the arm of the sofa and gazed up at him in a way that she thought must be how a rabbit stared in frozen panic at a hawk. Except that she wasn't frozen. She was hot, desire still warm and pulsing in her stomach. She wasn't really a rabbit either, she decided as she pushed herself up straight.

"Why did you do that?" she demanded, pulling at her sweater and wishing she could take it off.

"Didn't you like it?"

She glared at him. He knew she had liked it, so there wasn't much point in lying.

"It was very nice," she said with a forced little laugh. "But you said no strings——"

"I meant it too," he interrupted. "But when you told me about the sad gap my departure had left in the ranks of Pontglas's bachelors I felt it was only fair to make up for my untimely desertion." He gave her an exaggeratedly virtuous smile. "Do you really think I'm eligible, by the way?"

"Oh," gasped Bronwen. "Of all the arrogant, self-satisfied, patronizing——"

"Scoundrels?" suggested Slade helpfully.

Bronwen jumped to her feet. "I was going to say rats," she said viciously.

He nodded and slapped a hand pensively against his thigh. "And where do you think you're going?" he inquired.

"To bed."

"Ah. A woman after my own heart." He stood up.

"You're not coming with me," she cried, backing away. "You promised..."

"I suppose I did. But we've been through this before, haven't we? And I thought we established that rats don't keep promises." There was a hint of retribution in his eye as his arm snaked around her waist, and before she could escape he had her tightly trapped against his chest.

This time she did struggle. "Slade, let me go," she ordered.

"Certainly not. Rats don't." Ignoring her futile squirmings, he picked her up in both arms, kicked open the intervening door, and carried her into the bedroom.

When he dumped her down on the gold bedspread, and with one hand pinned both wrists lightly but very firmly above her head, she wriggled for a moment, and then screamed.

CHAPTER FOUR

SLADE, his feet still safely anchored on the floor, leaned over Bronwen and shifted his grasp.

"Am I still a rat?" he asked.

To her utter disbelief, he was grinning. A white, unabashedly wicked grin that didn't remind her of a rodent in the slightest.

Her body went limp with relief. And something else that she ruthlessly suppressed.

"You're only teasing me, aren't you?" she gasped. Her heart was still beating much too hard.

"Not at all. I'm punishing you for breaking our agreement and calling me names—after you specifically promised to behave with decent civility."

He released her wrists and sat down beside her on the bed.

Some punishment, thought Bronwen, running her eyes over his bare chest, and noting the tight stretch of fabric across his thighs. If he continued to sit there like that, half naked and sexy and mocking, it wouldn't take much to turn his punishment into a reward. Which later she would undoubtedly regret.

"I asked if I'm still a rat," he said, placing a hand on her neat tweed hip.

She stared into his deep blue eyes, and wondered what would happen if she said yes.

"No," she said after a while. "You broke your agreement too, and at the moment you remind me more of a wolf."

"Better, but still not flattering. Try again."

"Certainly not. Your ego's quite sufficiently inflated as it is."

He shook his head. "You don't learn, do you?" he murmured, once more reaching for her wrists.

Suddenly Bronwen was frightened. Not of him, but of herself. He was too close. His eyes were too blue, too demanding and seductive—and his fingers were closing around her arms. She had read of burning touches, and thought such phrases melodramatic nonsense. But there *was* heat where he touched her and she couldn't control the strength of her response. Slade was holding her very lightly, but the expression on his handsome face disturbed her. It was appraising, certainly, but at the same time hard and a little ruthless. He wouldn't hurt her, instinctively she knew that, but if she just put out a hand, touched the shining gold of his hair...

In the end it wasn't the hair on his head she touched, but the fine smooth silk on his chest.

At once his eyes narrowed, and she heard a sharp indrawn breath before he grabbed her hand and pushed it down by her side.

"I—I'm—what's the matter?" stammered Bronwen, confused and embarrassed and not at all sure what had happened.

Slade rose abruptly to his feet. "You're still the little innocent, aren't you?" he snapped, glaring down at her with a mixture of exasperation and incredulity.

Bronwen turned her head on the pillow so she couldn't see his half-naked torso, or the scornful lift to his lips. She didn't bother to answer him, because she wasn't all that innocent, and the currents that had swirled around them from the moment they had met again today weren't all that difficult to interpret. *She* didn't like him, *he* thought she was naive and stupid.

But both of them were in the grip of something her mother had referred to disapprovingly as "carnal lust." Well—maybe Slade wasn't. His feelings had never been an open book.

There was a silence between them that continued for several seconds. Then suddenly Bronwen felt his fingers in her hair, pushing it back over her shoulder.

"Good night, Michael's sister," he said in a voice that grated harshly on her ears. "Sleep well. The big bad wolf won't bite you yet."

"Just let him try," she retorted, her eyes firmly on the pale cream walls.

She heard him growl something that sounded like, "Don't tempt me," and then the door closed very quietly behind him.

Rat, thought Bronwen. I was right the first time.

She eased herself slowly off the bed and began to rifle through her suitcase in pursuit of a clean cotton nightgown. But by the time she had pulled it on, and been forced to start again because she'd forgotton to remove her blouse first, her state of mind was wavering somewhere between violent irritation and sheer panic. Some time ago, she remembered, she had seen a sign that read, "When in doubt, panic." Maybe she was on the right track.

Frowning, she thumped herself into the bed and pulled the sheets up. They were silk, which only increased her irritation, because such opulence served to remind her that Slade held all the best cards. And she was *damned* if she intended to panic. This was a ridiculous situation. All the same, Michael's welfare was what mattered, and as long as Slade kept his promise to keep his hands off her there was no reason why the current arrangement shouldn't work.

The only flaw in that conclusion was that Slade hadn't, in fact, kept his hands off her.

The moment she closed her eyes, and prepared to drift chastely off to sleep, unbidden and unwelcome came the knowledge that in some traitorous part of her being she didn't at all mind the touch of Slade's firm fingers...

She squeezed her eyes shut, turned on her side, and pushed the thought out of her mind.

"All right, lazy bones," drawled a voice that reached Bronwen through a haze of sleep. "I've pandered to your jet lag long enough. Up you get."

"Mmm? What...?" For a moment she couldn't remember where she was. "Jet lag...?"

"Forget it," ordered the voice. "I said, get up."

Oh. Now she remembered. She was in Slade's bed. Fortunately without Slade, who, when she raised her eyelids, was bending over her with a purposeful glint in his eye.

"I'm still tired," she mumbled, hoping he would go away.

"I dare say you are." The uncompromising reply was exactly what she might have expected. "But the best way to adjust to a time change is not to let it defeat you. You're in Vancouver now, and it happens to be ten in the morning."

"Why aren't you at work, then?" she asked, stalling.

"Because I don't choose to be, which is probably unfortunate for you."

Bronwen was inclined to agree with him, but she was wide-awake now, and there didn't seem much point to wasting any further time in bed. "If you'd care to leave the room, I'll get up,'' she said, in what she hoped was her most condescending voice.

But Slade wasn't an easy man to condescend to—especially when she was flat on her back in a cotton nightgown, and he was standing over her dressed in fawn colored trousers and a pale cream, very expensive-looking shirt. Casual attire for the rich and famous, thought Bronwen irritably—although she had to admit that he wore his clothes with a completely unconscious ease, and would probably look just as mouth-watering in faded jeans and a sweatshirt.

"But I'm not sure I *would* care to leave,'' he replied, eyeing her slim figure beneath the bedclothes. "I'd like to see the rest of that unprepossessing garment that makes the top half of you resemble my Victorian great-grandmother on a Sunday.''

"Why would you like to see it?'' demanded Bronwen. "I assure you the bottom half will leave just as much to your overworked imagination.''

He sighed. "I don't doubt it. Never mind, as we have a whole day ahead of us, I propose that we spend some of it purchasing a few improvements to your wardrobe.''

"We'll do no such thing,'' gasped Bronwen, sitting up quickly. "There's nothing wrong with my wardrobe.''

"Apart from the fact that green tweed is totally unsuited to the month of May, and that your nightgown belongs in a museum, you may be right,'' he agreed. "What else did you bring with you?''

Without waiting for an answer, he flung open the doors of a large walk-in cupboard and ran a practiced eye over her practical dresses and skirts. "Just as I thought,'' he said dismissively. "They won't do.''

"They'll do very well," snapped Bronwen, running *her* eye over the back of him as he stood before her meager wardrobe looking elegant, sexy and, because he was in her bedroom, very much the man on the make. In every sense of the phrase. He reminded her of a rich tycoon, carelessly offering frills to his mistress.

But he hadn't offered frills to Jenny. He hadn't been given the chance.

When he continued to stare disparagingly into the cupboard she said without pausing to think, "You may be in the habit of dressing up your women like dolls, Slade, but I'm not your woman——"

"And you're definitely not a doll," he finished for her, closing the door of the cupboard. "Don't worry, I doubt if decent clothes will turn you into one. And they certainly won't make you my woman." He leaned against the closed door and crossed his arms, surveying her through narrowed eyes as she lay with the covers pulled up almost to her nose.

Ridiculously Bronwen had a sudden vision of Jenny Price lying in a similar position, with a much younger Slade looking down at her. Her stomach gave a lurch, and because she was afraid of the signals her traitorous body might send his way she said furiously, "Get out. I don't want your gifts, and I don't want to be your woman."

"There's not much danger of that." He answered with a coldness that made her want to dive back under the covers. She was biting her lip, making up her mind to do just that, when she discovered that Slade was standing beside the bed. She felt his hands on her shoulders. "Come on," he said, his voice still cold and imperious. "Stop thinking up ways to insult me, and do as you're told and get up."

When Bronwen only glared at him he flung back the covers and hauled her onto her feet.

"Just as I thought," he said, holding her away from him as he took in her demure cotton nightgown with the dainty lace-collared neck. "Does it come with a chastity belt too?"

"As far as you're concerned, it does," snapped Bronwen. "Tell me, Slade, is this the way you usually treat your guests? Dragging them out of bed, making uncalled-for remarks about their clothes——?"

"Making uncalled-for remarks about their clothes, yes, sometimes," he interrupted with a mocking smile. "Usually along the lines of their being extraneous to the business at hand. But, to be honest, I believe this is the first occasion on which I've actually dragged a guest from my bed."

"I suppose you normally drag your ladyfriends *into* bed," scoffed Bronwen.

"Occasionally. But only if they're agreeable." His eyes glittered, piercing her with their bright intensity. "Are *you* agreeable, Bronwen? We could postpone the shopping for a while." He ran a finger lightly down her spine, spreading his palm so briefly over her flimsily clad bottom that she wasn't even sure she had felt it.

"No," she gasped, knowing that at this moment it wasn't true, and that if he touched her again she would let him drag her to the ends of the earth. She stepped back hastily, until her calves came up against the bed. "No, Slade. I want you to go away. Now." When he didn't move she gritted her teeth and added, "Please."

He nodded, the planes of his face flat and enigmatic. "That's what I thought you'd say. And, since you said please so nicely . . . all right, Michael's sister,

you win. At least for the moment. Hurry up—
breakfast is waiting.''

It was only after he had gone that Bronwen saw the
ceramic tray beside her bed, complete with a pot of
coffee, a blue cup and saucer, a bowl of sugar and a
jug of milk.

She blinked. Slade, for all his dictatorial ways, had
actually had sufficient consideration for her weariness
to make coffee. She poured some and took a quick
sip. It wasn't bad either. She shook her head, wondering if Slade was really as contradictory as he
seemed, or whether he was deliberately going out of
his way to confuse her.

If it was the latter, when it came to a decision on
what to wear, he had succeeded brilliantly.

She stared glumly at the selection of Pontglas skirts,
and at the two prim shirtwaisted dresses. The pale
green with the gold buttons had always been one of
her favorites. But now, in light of Slade's scathing
comments, it seemed faded and a bit dowdy.

Defiantly she tugged it off the hanger and put it
on.

Slade was lounging at the table, reading the paper,
when she finally stopped putting off the evil moment
and went to join him.

"Good morning," he said politely.

"You've already seen me," said Bronwen.

"I know. I'm making a fresh start. I have a feeling
you didn't appreciate my company the first time
around."

"I didn't."

"Mmm." He gazed pensively at the pale green
dress, and Bronwen stiffened defensively. But he only
jerked his head in the direction of the kitchen and

said peremptorily, "I made pancakes. Help yourself." He went on reading the paper.

After a startled pause Bronwen shrugged and walked over to the stove, where she found three congealed pancakes lying cold and neglected on a plate. She smothered a smile as her gaze fell on an open box of pancake mix and a pile of dirty crockery in the sink. Slade hadn't been deceiving her when he'd said he didn't like cooking.

She heated the pancakes in the microwave, which made them soggy and warm instead of cold and congealed, and carried them back to the table.

"Thank you," she said, making an effort to restore some sort of amity. "It was nice of you to make coffee. And—er—breakfast."

"Which, I gather, fails to impress you," he said dryly. "Just as well, because it's not a service I normally provide. Tomorrow you can make me scrambled eggs—with bacon and fried potatoes on the side."

"Which is not a service *I* normally provide," said Bronwen tartly.

"Then it's time you started." He turned a page and folded the paper neatly.

"Slade," she said, glaring at the sharp angle of his jaw, "I don't know why you brought me here, but if it was just because you needed an unpaid servant you can think again."

He lowered the paper deliberately. "You know, I hadn't thought of that," he said, feigning surprise. "However, now that you're here . . ."

"Now that I'm here, I am *not* going to be at your beck and call."

"I didn't ask you to be." He no longer sounded quite so cool and amused. "If you must know, I brought you here because I owe it to Michael's sister, to the gentle little girl with the sweet smile who always tried to smooth over troubled waters. However, I see now that that child no longer exists." He gave her a look she was unable to interpret. "In any case, *I* have work to do while you're with me, and I see no reason why I shouldn't expect you to perform the occasional domestic chore. Or is that too much to ask?"

Put like that, or, rather, if he had put it nicely, it *wasn't* too much to ask. If only he hadn't such a talent for putting her back up...

"You're not working now," she pointed out.

"I'm taking the day off. No doubt I'll pay for it tomorrow when I discover that my entire staff has enjoyed a holiday as well."

"Are you trying to make me feel guilty?" demanded Bronwen.

"Is that possible?"

"Yes, of course it is..." She broke off as she noticed a sardonic curl lifting the corner of his mouth. "Of course it's possible," she finished, exasperated. "All right, Slade, *you* win this time. I'll make breakfast tomorrow."

"I knew you would," he replied, turning back to his paper.

Bronwen finished the last bite of tepid pancake, and wondered whether arsenic was still in fashion. Failing that, salt in his coffee might do as well.

Slade paid no attention when she started to clear the table. Bronwen pursed her lips and made a great production of stacking dirty dishes in the dishwasher. She didn't mind the work, but it annoyed her that he seemed to take it for granted. She glanced at his bright head bent studiously over the paper. To be fair, he wasn't used to clearing up after himself. He probably paid Mrs. Doyle a good wage. On the other hand, *she* wasn't Mrs. Doyle.

In the end she went on tidying the kitchen for her own sake because, like her mother before her, she had never been able to abide a messy house.

"Nice job." Slade nodded approvingly when she put the last dish away and began to dry her hands on a towel. "I may even keep you."

"You won't get the chance."

"Don't be too sure of that." He pushed himself back from the table and rose with a leisurely grace that, briefly, before she remembered, made her long to reach out and touch him. "Now," he went on, "seeing that you've finished your domestic duties, I suggest we make a start on today's program."

"What program?" Bronwen scowled at him, prepared to object to whatever he might have in mind. *Her* domestic duties, indeed! After she'd cleaned up *his* kitchen.

But he left her no time for objections. "You'll see," he said. "Come on, we've wasted enough time as it is." He was already opening the door. "Where's your sweater?"

"In the bedroom." She left him twisting the handle impatiently.

Standing in front of the big cupboard, she deliberately chose the oldest and least attractive cardigan she could find—a baggy navy blue that had once been home to a family of hungry moths. If Slade insisted on organizing her day she would go along with him. She hadn't a lot else to do. But there was no way she was going to let him dictate what she wore.

Slade grimaced when she reappeared, but he said nothing as he opened the door and ushered her into the elevator.

"Where are we going?" she demanded when they reached the bottom. "Don't forget, I have to see Michael——"

"I'm not likely to forget," he replied. "First things first."

"Michael *is* first."

"To your mind, maybe. Not to mine."

She looked up, startled by the abrasive edge to his voice. His face was unusually hard too. She shook her head, wondering what had got into him now. Michael was Slade's friend, and yet sometimes, when he spoke of him, she had the impression that he bore her brother some deep-seated grudge.

A short time later the Porsche pulled into a parking spot in front of what appeared to be a very smart boutique. The kind with one improbably elegant, and presumably priceless, garment draped tastefully over a svelte model in the window.

"Slade," said Bronwen warningly. "I said you weren't buying my clothes."

"I know you did. And please don't say it again. It's beginning to bore me." Wasting no further words, he opened the car door, pulled her out and towed her across the pavement.

"Slade, you can't—I won't..."

"I can, and I will." His mouth was stretched in a twisted, scornful grimace. "Surely it's the least I can do. Just because I didn't do right by Jenny doesn't mean I can't do right by you."

Bronwen frowned. His words didn't ring quite true. In any case, although he was generously providing her with a temporary roof over her head, he was making no effort to make her feel comfortable and at home. Quite the contrary. He seemed to be taking a perverse pleasure in baiting her, in making her feel ignorant and young, and jeering at her natural concern for the woman he had abandoned so cruelly. She pressed the palms of her hands flat against her sides. All right. She'd show him! If he wanted to assert his authority by overhauling her wardrobe she would let him—and take her own perverse pleasure in spending his money. Lots of it. He wouldn't miss it, and it was the only way she could think of to take the wind out of his sails.

Straightening her shoulders, she gave him a brittle smile, and marched past him into the shop.

A tall, glamorous woman in black advanced toward them with a cultivated smile. When she saw Slade the cultivated smile changed to one of familiarity. "Slade," she purred. "Darling, it's been too long——"

"Two weeks, I believe," Slade interrupted. "And, if I remember correctly, there was some little problem about a husband."

The woman in black giggled. "Well, yes. So tiresome. Maybe another time, darling."

"And maybe not," said Slade shortly. "Valerie, this is Miss Evans. She is in dire need of some suitable clothes."

As Bronwen scowled up at him the woman called Valerie ran a perfunctory but professional eye over her customer's plain green dress. "I see what you mean," she drawled, looking down her nose in a way that Bronwen suspected was meant to discompose a potential rival. "Yes." She put a finger over her lips. "Something simple. Very well cut. Not too clinging. And not green."

"But I always wear green."

"Precisely." For the first time Bronwen detected a trace of a British accent in the woman's voice. She wondered if Slade had known her long. No, probably not. He had said something about an unexpected husband . . .

She lifted her chin and announced flatly, "I like green."

"Unoriginal." Valerie dismissed the objection with a careless wave of her hand, and shot a glance of amused complicity at Slade. "Redheads wear far too much green. Now you, Miss Evans, would suit cream with a touch of gold. Or perhaps this mauve." She pointed to a dress in a style that Bronwen would never even have dreamed of trying on, let alone buying.

"But that's not my——" Bronwen began.

"If Valerie says it is you can take her word for it," cut in Slade. "She's the best in the business."

I'll bet, thought Bronwen, remembering the husband. The question is, *what* business? Her eyes lighted with a smoky glare that her friends had learned to beware of. "Very well, Slade," she said sweetly. "Whatever you say."

As Bronwen followed Valerie to a change room at the back Slade's eyebrows drew thoughtfully together. There was something altogether too compliant about Miss Evans's capitulation. He didn't trust it, and, although his memories of Bronwen were of a gentle, biddable little thing, the reality had proved very different. She'd been under his skin from the moment he'd first seen her again in the hospital corridor. Not that he was particularly proud of his own behavior. And not, he thought grimly, that she wasn't capable of holding her own. That, he supposed, was what made her such a challenge and a provocation.

In the elegant brass-fitted change room, Bronwen tried on everything Valerie suggested, and airily agreed to take the lot.

The older woman didn't speak much as the boxes continued to pile up, and Bronwen had a feeling that, although she wouldn't compromise her professional reputation by suggesting the wrong clothes to a customer, she would very much like to be free to suggest sackcloth and elastic on this occasion.

She didn't, though, and gradually Bronwen came to see that Slade was right. These clothes had flair, gave her the modern sophistication she had lacked. Especially the cream silk with the gold trim.

It was the last thing she tried on, sleek and elegant with its low-cut neck and softly flaring skirt.

"Show that one to Slade," said Valerie with a bitter little grimace. "He's been waiting so patiently that it's only fair to give him a preview of what he's paying for."

"He's not paying for me," said Bronwen sharply. She hadn't missed the snide innuendo.

"Of course not." The smile subsided into a smirk, and Bronwen knew Valerie didn't believe her.

"Is Slade an old friend of yours?" she asked casually.

Valerie gave a high-pitched laugh. "In a manner of speaking. Slade has a lot of friends. Go on, show him the dress."

A lot of friends . . . yes, no doubt he had. She could imagine what sort of friends, too, if the glamorous Valerie was any kind of example.

Bronwen wasn't sure why Valerie was so insistent that she model for Slade. It was obvious that she resented his interest in a woman she regarded as a rival. So either she was a masochist, or else she couldn't resist showing off her expertise—because there was no doubt the dress was sensational.

"Go on," Valerie urged. "Slade has impeccable taste—in women's clothing."

But not in women, was the implication Bronwen didn't fail to catch.

It didn't matter. Slade's love life wasn't her concern. And she couldn't wait to see his face when he saw those boxes.

Arranging a cool little smile on her face, she strolled out onto the shop floor, turned slowly, and came to a stop a few feet from where he was sprawled in a low armchair, which seemed much too small for his lean frame. As usual, he looked mouth-watering.

"Do you like it?" she asked, pirouetting.

"Keep still," he ordered.

There was something in his tone that made her do as he said, and when she looked at his face and saw his gaze moving over her in a warm, unhurried appraisal that did uncomfortable things to her stomach, she found herself holding her breath.

"I asked if you liked it," she repeated when he didn't speak.

"Yes," he said finally, his deep baritone curling round her like silk. "The package is quite irresistible. I can hardly wait to unwrap it."

Bronwen let her breath out in a rush. "You'll not be unwrapping it," she said hotly. And then, summoning all her reserves of dignity, "I've chosen a few other things as well." She waved at the stack of boxes that Valerie was piling beside him, and waited for the anticipated explosion.

It didn't come. Instead she saw his eyebrows lift just a fraction and a quick smile flicker across his face.

"I see you learn fast," he remarked dryly. "That's most encouraging. Thank you, Valerie, we'll take them."

"Miss Evans has a rather—*youthful* figure," murmured Valerie. "But I hope you'll agree we've done our best."

"Your best is very good, and you know it," Slade told her brusquely. "And Miss Evans's figure is very much to my taste."

"It's also *mine*," Bronwen pointed out irritably. "Would you mind not discussing it as if I'm a prize cow, or some pig you're picking out at the county fair?"

Slade put his head to one side, and she saw that his eyes were bright with suppressed amusement. "No," he said judiciously after a short, contemplative pause, "no, I don't think so."

"What don't you think?" she asked, taken aback.

"That you are at all what I'd select if I was in the market for a cow or a pig at the county fair."

He gave her a grin of such wolfish admiration that Bronwen almost fell off her high horse and laughed. But she managed not to, and went to change back into the green dress with a toss of her head and a smile that was meant to be supercilious.

Slade thought it was sweet and self-conscious and quite charming.

A few minutes later, feeling curiously deflated, she followed him out to the car. As they drove off Valerie called, "Goodbye, darlings. Have a wonderful night." She swayed back into the shop, smiling a maliciously arch little smile.

"What did she mean by that?" asked Bronwen unwisely.

"Exactly what you think she meant, my dear. That you and I are going to enjoy a glorious night of passion in my king-size bed. An appealing proposition, I must say. I don't much like sleeping on the sofa."

"Oh, don't you?" said Bronwen through her teeth, conscious that a familiar outrage was turning her face bright pink. She knew that her reaction was exacerbated by the fact that she felt guilty about deliberately wasting his money. Still, that didn't stop her announcing firmly, "Slade, I've had enough. Take me back to your apartment at once, please. I'm leaving to find a place on my own."

"If you insist I'll take you back to my apartment," he replied equably. "But you're not leaving."

"You'll have to hold me there by force, then."

"That can be arranged."

She thought about grabbing the wheel and forcing the car to a stop, but there was a lot of traffic on the road, and she hadn't yet reached the point where she was willing to risk life and limb in order to escape from Slade's clutches.

"Why?" she asked, her voice shaking. "Why are you doing this, Slade? I'm not Jenny Price. And I'm not one of your Valeries either, if that's why you bought me all those clothes."

"We won't discuss Jenny Price," he said, with such harsh severity that Bronwen jumped. "And what do you mean by that incomparable phrase, 'One of my Valeries'?" His leather-gloved hand curled around the wheel.

"It's obvious, isn't it?" Bronwen glared at a passing cyclist. "Valerie was your mistress—until an inconvenient husband intervened. You haven't changed at all, have you, Slade?" When she glanced at his profile she saw that his mouth had hardened. She didn't like the way his fingers gripped the wheel either. They reminded her too much of talons.

"No," he said. "I haven't changed." He turned his head briefly so that she caught the white flash of his teeth. "But, if you must know, Valerie was nothing so old-fashioned as my mistress. She *has* been a casual acquaintance for some time. When I took her out a few weeks ago at her suggestion our conversation was interrupted by a husband whose existence I wasn't aware of. He seemed more resigned than dismayed, though. Valerie, as perhaps you noticed, was more annoyed than repentant." He swung the wheel sharply to the right. "It may disappoint you to know that I prefer my women unattached."

"Like Jenny Price?" asked Bronwen with acid on her breath. She hated him like this. All cold-blooded and jeering and callous.

Slade's hand jerked on the wheel and they narrowly missed an oncoming car. "No," he said, with a violence so coldly contained that it made her flinch. "*Not* like Jenny Price. Jenny was a sweet kid. Contrary to your charming opinion of me, I wish her well."

"Generous of you, in the circumstances." Bronwen made no effort to hide her contempt.

She expected Slade to hit back with some slashing retort, but to her bewilderment he only tightened his jaw and said with a total lack of emphasis, "It is, isn't it? And now, if you don't mind, we'll abandon the absorbing subject of my private life which, by the way, is absolutely none of your business, and concentrate on beautiful Vancouver."

He's done it again, thought Bronwen. Made me feel in the wrong, even though this whole situation is his doing. And those boxes are going back to Valerie at the first opportunity I get. I was out of my mind to accept them.

But deep down she had a disquieting feeling that she'd been more or less out of her mind from the moment Slade had come back into her life.

"All right," she said with weary resignation, because there didn't seem any good reason to object and she was tired of fighting, "I'll be a good tourist."

For the rest of the day they maintained a sort of wary truce while Slade took her to all the best-known tourist spots, and even made an effort not to look as though he'd done it all a hundred times before.

It wasn't until late in the afternoon that hostilities were resumed with a vengeance, and it happened when Bronwen had relaxed her guard and given up anticipating trouble.

"I suppose," Slade said as they were making their way back from the Capilano Dam, which rose in concrete majesty beneath the mountains to supply Vancouver with water, "that you want to see the suspension bridge next."

"Should I?" asked Bronwen.

"If you want to scare yourself silly, yes, you should."

Bronwen noted the patronizing arch of his eyebrows and felt a familiar spark of irritation. "I don't mind heights," she told him, lifting her chin. When he looked loftily disbelieving she added sharply, "You're confusing me with Jenny, perhaps. *She's* the one who's always been scared of heights."

Slade stood perfectly still. They had just reached the concrete parking lot, and for a moment Bronwen was appalled by the look in his eyes. At first she thought it was hurt; then she realized it was just plain fury, as his fists bunched up against his thighs and the muscles in his neck pulled into corded rope.

She took a quick step backward. "I didn't mean..." Her voice trailed off, because he was no longer beside her but striding ahead to the car.

She climbed in when he flung the door open for her, and after one look at his face decided that silence was the better part of apology. Not that she had much to apologize for, she reminded herself. Slade deserved all he got on the subject of Jenny Price. Still, she *had* half promised to keep her opinions to herself. And there was something about his reaction that didn't altogether add up...

Five minutes later, and without a word, Slade paid for them to enter the wooded park which advertised itself as the home of the famous Capilano Suspension Bridge.

"It's a very long way down," Bronwen ventured, peering down the rocky tree-lined canyon, which was spanned by a noticeably swaying bridge held up by cables.

"You don't have to cross if you'd rather not." Slade stared straight ahead, not looking at her.

"Of course I'll cross," she said, heading for the steps leading down to the bridge and not bothering to check that he was following. She could do without his company for a moment. When she reached the middle she stopped, enjoying the gentle sway as she stared down at the river that from this height seemed no wider than a stream. She glanced back, couldn't see Slade, and carried on to the opposite side.

When Slade still didn't appear she concluded that he was avoiding her company too. He'd been in a very black humor since her untimely reference to Jenny's fear of heights.

Bronwen began a leisurely stroll along the woodland trail, relishing the spongy softness beneath her feet, and taking time to inspect the unfamiliar ferns and foliage.

Half an hour or so later she wandered back, still taking her time, and stopping once more on the bridge to stare down at the water cascading over the rocks far below. When she reached the park again Slade was nowhere to be seen.

She meandered into the gift shop. He didn't seem to be there either.

Oh, dear, she thought. Perhaps he's decided to abandon me. Then she was annoyed with herself because the idea wasn't as appealing as she'd expected. She picked up a small fake argillite carving of a seal.

"And where the hell," said a furious voice behind her, "do you think you've been?"

"Walking," she replied woodenly. "Where were you?"

Strong hands on her shoulders spun her around, and she put the seal down hastily.

"I," said Slade, "have been searching all over hell's half acre for you."

"Why? I was all right."

"Oh, were you? And how was I to know that? I saw you reach the end of the bridge, and then you disappeared on me."

Staring at him, her indignation rising by the minute, Bronwen was reminded of her father lecturing her for being late home from school. He'd worn just that expression of anger because his authority had been flouted, mixed with genuine concern for her welfare.

"I wasn't gone that long," she pointed out. "You could have come too."

"I did. And I have spent the last hour looking for you. Don't you realize people have fallen over these cliffs——?"

"The trails are quite well marked," Bronwen interrupted. "I'm not a complete idiot, Slade."

He took a deep breath, and several people stared at them curiously.

"No," he said viciously. "No, I'm the idiot. My life would be a whole lot less complicated if you *had* broken your beautiful neck."

"There was never any danger of that."

He pulled out a handkerchief and wiped his forehead. His face, Bronwen noted, was very pale.

"Slade," she said quietly, "I don't understand."

"No," he snapped. "You wouldn't."

She frowned. "Then . . ."

He grabbed her elbow, and she let him tow her out of the shop. "Once in two days is enough," he grated when he got her outside.

"What does that mean?"

"It means that reading of your death in the paper was more than enough excitement for one week. I didn't enjoy my trip to the hospital to tell Michael his sister had died." The words were still harsh, bitten off, but he sounded less explosive now. She no longer expected to find herself slung across his shoulder and dumped into the car like some wayward child.

"Oh. Michael," she said. Of course. He had been worried about *Michael's* feelings. Why had she ever thought his concern might be for her?

"Yes, Michael. Your brother."

Bronwen nodded. There didn't seem much to say. "I'm sorry you were worried," she managed stonily.

"Not that worried," he replied with an edge to his voice. "You happen to be my responsibility, that's all."

Bronwen thought she was her own responsibility, but she decided to let it go.

"Where are we going?" she asked as they passed a row of cars and sped off down the hill.

"To the place where I go when my spirit needs healing and my heart is in need of refreshment." The words were almost lyrical, but he spoke them with a bitterness that made her flinch.

"Oh," she said. "Slade—I really am sorry that...that I upset you. I had no idea you'd be anxious."

"What makes you think I was anxious?" When she didn't answer he added without looking at her, "I was a steeplejack at one time. My partner was killed in a fall."

Bronwen, appalled by the brutally flat statement, whispered, "Oh, dear Lord. I didn't know..."

"Why should you? Just don't take off on me again. Do you understand?"

In any other circumstances she would have told him she wasn't a dog to be kept beside him on a leash. As it was, she said nothing.

Slade didn't speak either as he drove on into town. It was almost as if he'd forgotten she was there.

About half an hour later they pulled up beside an unusual white-walled enclosure topped by dark, moon-shaped eaves. A sign proclaimed that they had arrived at "The Dr. Sun Yat-Sen Classical Chinese Garden."

Still without speaking, Slade led her through a doorway into a courtyard paved in intricate patterns of pebbles. When she moved Bronwen's gaze was drawn to a jade green pool, from which an island built of pitted limestone rose like a surrealistic mountain. There were plants too—pine, bamboo and plum, and others which she couldn't identify.

Glancing at Slade's face, Bronwen saw that all the lines of anger were smoothed out now, and she felt a surprising sense of tranquillity.

"What strange, tortured-looking rocks," she murmured, staring across to the island. "They look like dragons, and horses and fish and—oh, anything I want to imagine."

"Mmm," said Slade. "That's the idea. They come from the bottom of Lake Tai, near Suzhou. This garden is modeled on the private classical gardens of the Ming dynasty, and it's the only one of its kind outside China."

"It's lovely," said Bronwen simply.

"Yes," agreed Slade, watching her rapt expression. "Did you know that, in Taoist philosophy, everything is based on the principle of yin and yang?"

"Yin and yang?"

"The two forces of cosmic harmony. Here you have hard rock and soft bamboo that moves in the wind, sunlight and shadow, light balanced by dark." He rested a hand on her shoulder. "Man by woman. Nature's harmony. Those old Taoist philosophers knew what they were about."

"Perhaps," said Bronwen, thinking that there wasn't much harmony about her and Slade. She listened to the bright sound of a miniature waterfall, saw the reflected images of plants and trees, and in the distance the Pavilion of Jade Green Waters. "It *is* peaceful." She touched his arm. "Why did you bring me here, Slade?"

"Because it's where I come when the world seems out of kilter. Here, once you change your perspective you change your view of the universe. Just like life. There's no fear, and no boredom for the eyes either. Only refreshment and pleasure for the heart. We all need that sometimes.''

Bronwen looked up at him, finding it hard to reconcile this sober, reflective Slade with the dynamic, moving force she was used to. Obviously there were many sides to this man. Sometimes he seemed as mysterious as the opaque green water.

But she was glad he had brought her here. She no longer felt as though she were balanced on the edge of a precipice ready to drop into the unknown.

Even so, she couldn't quite shake the feeling that this respite from tension was temporary.

They were back in Slade's apartment, after a lengthy visit to Michael, before it occurred to Bronwen that his motive in taking her to the Chinese garden might not have been as simple as she imagined.

Man and woman, he had said. Separate entities, yet part of a natural completeness . . .

Across the room Slade was efficiently uncorking champagne . . .

''Slade?'' She frowned. ''What are you doing?''

''Ending the day on what I hope will be a celebratory note,'' he answered lightly.

''How celebratory?'' she asked, her uneasiness needing no explanation.

When his nostrils flared in that intimidating way she was getting used to she suspected she had asked the wrong question.

She had.

''Bronwen Evans,'' he said, in a clipped voice, ''I believe I've told you before that I'm very tired of being treated like Henry the Eighth on the prowl for a seventh wife to bed and behead——''

"You mentioned Caligula, actually," she interrupted. "And Henry only beheaded two wives."

"Very forbearing of him," muttered Slade. "I'm beginning to feel a certain sympathy for old Henry." He poured champagne into a narrow glass and handed it to her.

After a moment's hesitation, she took it.

"To Henry," he said, raising his glass.

Bronwen choked, and almost spilled her champagne. "No," she said, recovering herself. "To Michael and his speedy recovery."

"Hmm." Heavy lids shielded his eyes, hiding any clue to his thoughts. "If you insist. To Michael."

She wondered if she was imagining the note of grim resignation in his voice.

To her relief he made no attempt to capitalize on the champagne, nor did he make any further reference to his bed. Instead he kicked his shoes off and sat down to concentrate on the crossword. Although she breathed a little more freely, she was disturbed to feel a faint stab of disappointment.

They passed the remainder of the evening sitting side by side on the sofa with the papers, in a more or less amicable silence, punctuated by occasional attempts on Bronwen's part to apologize for accepting the clothes.

The fourth time she assured him that she meant to send them back Slade threw down the crossword and said, "Right. That does it."

"What's the matter?" Bronwen gasped as he leaned toward her.

He paused with his hand on her knee. "It seems to me," he said, in a tone that sent quivers up her spine, "that you feel some compelling need to pay for those dresses. I'm about to see to it that you do."

CHAPTER FIVE

"WH—WHAT?" Bronwen shrank back against the sea green cushions, her gray eyes widening with shock. "What are you talking about, Slade?"

"I'm talking about your deplorable habit of dwelling on the subject of a few dresses—none of which you are wearing, I could point out."

"But I can't wear them. I told you, I'm taking them back. I . . ." She paused and then took the plunge. "I only allowed you to buy them for me to pay you back for being so overbearing and bossy. But it was wrong of me. Childish. I shouldn't have done it."

"No," he said. "Perhaps you shouldn't. But, since you did, and since you're bent on being a complete bore about it, it's time you found out just exactly how bossy I can be."

"What do you mean?" She brushed a hair nervously out of her eyes, and wished he'd take his hand off her knee. It made her feel hot and flustered, and curiously unlike her normal self.

"I mean you're going to pay me for those dresses." He drew back suddenly and stretched himself out on the sofa. "Come on." He opened his arms. "Kiss me."

"Certainly not," said Bronwen, sitting up very straight.

"I said kiss me."

"No."

He smiled, a long, contemplative smile, that made her gulp. "But you'd like to, wouldn't you?"

"Of course not."

"Are you sure?" He trailed a bare foot suggestively along her nylon-clad thigh.

Bronwen gasped. "Slade—don't."

"Then do as you're told, Miss Evans."

"Told?" repeated Bronwen stupidly. She couldn't think straight while he was lying there looking so lean and desirable, with his long, muscular body rippling with male strength and vitality. It made her want to—to...

"Bronwen, my dear, don't make me prove to you how overbearing I am." His voice was soft, sensuous and coercive—and, without being wholly aware of what she was doing, she lifted her hand and laid it over his knee.

Through eyes that weren't totally focused she saw Slade draw a quick breath. "That's better," he said quietly. "Now, if you'll just come a little closer——"

"Said the spider to the fly," she whispered shakily.

Slade smiled. "I'm not sure I like the analogy, but if you want to put it like that..." He rubbed his toe down her thigh again, and Bronwen groaned and gave up.

The moment she bent toward him Slade raised his arms and pulled her down on top of him. She could feel his heart beating through the smooth silky fabric of his shirt.

"Kiss me," he murmured. His voice was husky, and Bronwen, who was in the grip of the wildest, most abandoned craving she had ever known, moved her lips from his cheek and kissed him full on the mouth.

His arms tightened, and she felt his palms move caressingly over her back, and down lower. Then they spread out over the skimpy green cotton below her waist.

"Slade, oh, Slade," she murmured, lifting her head. "Please..."

"Kiss me some more," he commanded.

She needed no urging, and this time when she lowered her lips over his he responded with a fierce passion that would have made her cry out if she'd been able.

As his tongue forced her lips apart and began a ruthless exploration of her mouth her hand moved to his neck, began to fumble clumsily with his shirt buttons...

"Hell!"

So suddenly that she scarcely realized it had happened Bronwen found herself pushed upright. Slade, with a face like summer thunder, sat up too, and, with his elbows resting on his knees, supported his forehead on his fists.

"What the hell do you think you were doing?" he growled, not looking at her.

Bronwen didn't know what she'd been doing. Whatever it was, Slade had started it, and he had no cause to be blaming her now. She made a concentrated effort to dampen the heat still curling and surging in her stomach, and said frigidly, "I'm not at all sure, but I must have temporarily taken leave of my senses. I think a more pertinent question might be, 'Why did you break your promise not to touch me?'"

"I didn't touch you."

She lifted a hand to her mouth. "Slade, how can you sit there and tell such ridiculous lies?"

"I'm not." He sat up then, and looked straight at her. "If you'll remember, I said that, in order to stop your constant harping on about those dresses, I'd make you pay for them. Which I did. I didn't touch you, Bronwen. You touched me."

It was true in a way, but what woman could be proof against the potent force of Slade's sexuality when he chose to turn it up to full power?

"All right, then," she said dully. "So you've proved you can get exactly what you want. But you didn't."

"Really? How do you know I didn't?"

"Well..." She moistened her lips. "I thought..." She tried again. "Are you telling me you spent all that money on me for nothing more than a kiss?"

"Nothing more than...? Ah. I see. What a little cynic you are, Bronwen." He touched her cheek lightly and stood up. "Didn't it occur to you that I might choose to buy things for you with no other motive than to see you looking nice, and suitably dressed for what promises to be a long hot summer?"

"No," said Bronwen. "It didn't. You've always looked out for yourself, Slade—and it's not easy to forget about the past."

"The past be damned," he said harshly. "What do you know about it, little village girl?"

Bronwen inched back against the arm of the sofa, aghast at the sudden storm she had conjured up, and stunned by the blazing blue fury in his eyes.

"Slade, please——"

"But I don't please," he said gratingly, placing long fingers over her shoulder, and staring down at her like an eagle trying to decide which portion of its prey to devour first. When his thumbs began to press a little too hard she flinched.

A look of utter frustration passed over his features then, a sort of baffled hopelessness, and he released her with a muffled exclamation that she was glad she wasn't able to understand.

"Oh, go to bed," he said roughly.

When she only sat still, gaping at him, he repeated, "Go on. Go to bed. I have work to get on with. And in the morning don't forget I want scrambled eggs."

"And bacon," muttered Bronwen, too shattered and confused to tell him he would be able to count himself lucky if he got lumpy, arsenic-flavored porridge and burnt toast. That news could wait until morning. At the moment she was more than happy to retire to bed, as he suggested. Provided he didn't intend to join her.

She eyed him doubtfully.

"No," he said, accurately guessing her thoughts. "Provided I hear not one further word about those dresses, you're quite safe."

She wasn't, though, she thought despairingly as she pulled on the nightgown that he said belonged in a museum. How could she possibly be safe with Slade in the next room, undoubtedly plotting further assaults on her peace of mind? And body, she made herself add quickly.

Never in a million years would she have expected him to have had such a devastating effect on her body. Which was all it was, she told herself firmly. A serious case of unrequited lust. And the best way to deal with it was to get as far away as possible from its source. Not easy, as long as Michael remained in the hospital. True, he was well on the road to recovery, but until he was on his feet again she really didn't want to leave Vancouver.

Bronwen tossed her head restlessly. She could certainly leave Slade's apartment, though. Staying here had seemed a reasonable enough arrangement at one point, but, as she had found out to her cost, reason didn't enter the picture much once Slade had his mind set on a course.

Which meant the only solution was to get away. Tomorrow. As soon as he left to go to work.

With that in mind, she decided it would be best not to arouse his suspicions, so when she heard his alarm screech at 6:00 a.m. she stumbled quickly out of bed.

Too quickly. Slade was in the living room, wearing only a very brief pair of shorts.

"Excuse me," she gasped, flushing and backing away. "I—I was going to get your breakfast, but..."

"In that case, I certainly won't excuse you," he replied briskly. "Go right ahead." He made no attempt to cover himself as Bronwen, averting her eyes, scurried past him into the kitchen.

"That bad?" she heard his voice jeer gently from behind her. "I know I'm not at my best in the morning, but..." The words trailed off in smothered laughter as Bronwen slammed a frying pan onto the stove, and only just avoided flattening her thumb.

Not at his best in the morning, indeed, she thought furiously. He was absolutely glorious in the morning. Which was why it was altogether unfair of him to wander around looking like that.

She busied herself with eggs, bacon and toast, and paid no further attention to Slade until he came into the kitchen, fully dressed in a formidable gray suit that made him look intimidatingly cold and forbidding. Bronwen decided she wouldn't like to be on the opposing side in any of his business negotiations.

"By the way," he said as he pulled out a chair and waited with irritating expectation to be served, "don't bother going into hiding the moment my back is turned, will you? I have sources at Michael's hospital. It would be quite a simple matter to find you if you disappeared. No." He held up his hand as Bronwen lifted a plate of eggs from the counter with the obvious intention of aiming it at his head. "I wouldn't do that. I always return punches—and flying eggs."

When she dumped the plate down in front of him with a sound that he suspected was caused by grinding teeth he laughed and reached out to catch her by the hand.

"Don't sulk," he said softly. "It makes you look like a trout. Besides, even if you don't believe it yet, I really do have your interests at heart. Hotels don't come cheap in Vancouver."

"I'm not without funds," said Bronwen stiffly.

"I'm sure you're not, but you ought to save your— *funds*, for emergencies. What if Michael has a relapse?"

She hadn't thought of that. She had left home in too much of a rush to worry about long-term planning. And Slade was being nice for a change. If only he would stay like this, instead of going all domineering and bossy and—there was no getting away from it—sexy.

"Promise you won't cause me all kinds of unnecessary trouble by running away," he said, smiling with such seductive persuasion that she lost sight of her reason for wanting to run away in the first place. "And promise you'll shut up about those clothes."

"Yes," she said, battling an unnervingly limp sensation in her legs. "I promise."

"Good." He patted her absently on the white terrytowel rear of her robe, and went on eating his breakfast.

Bronwen shivered and hurried back to the kitchen.

"Bloody man," she said out loud the moment the door closed behind him.

She rarely swore, and in fact Slade hadn't been especially bloody this morning, but she was confused, unsure of herself, and muddle always made her prickly. She looked at the kitchen clock and saw that it was only 8:00 a.m. Much too early to visit Michael. Frowning, she padded into the bedroom and began to unpack yesterday's boxes.

The pale blue jumpsuit, she decided. Valerie had insisted Slade would approve of that. Forgetting that pleasing Slade wasn't on her list of things to do, she put it on. Staring at herself in the mirror, she was surprised to see how stylish it made her look. She shrugged uncomfortably, still not feeling right that she had been maneuvered into keeping these clothes. She would have to do something to make it up to Slade, whether he wanted her to or not—and not to please him, but herself.

For want of anything better to do, she wandered into the bathroom and started to scrub out the sink. Although Slade's living room was relatively neat and tidy, she had noticed piles of discarded clothing in the bedroom, and the bathroom was in need of a good cleaning. On top of that, the striped green wallpaper above the tiles was beginning to peel.

"Hmm," she murmured, pulling at the paper and watching it come easily away. "I wonder . . ."

An hour later she was standing at the kitchen counter with a pencil and a ruler, making confident marks on a brand-new roll of wallpaper. An hour after that, working with a restless energy that only surfaced when she was particularly upset about something, she was plastering the paper efficiently to the bathroom wall.

When only a few more feet remained to be covered she made herself stop to check the time. Bother. She'd have to finish the job later. Michael would be waiting for her visit.

She was late, so she called the taxi number Slade had left her, and was amazed when the driver told her the fare had already been paid. Slade again, she thought, not sure whether to be grateful or resentful of his high-handedness.

"Wow," said Michael as soon as she entered the ward. "What's happened to you, Bron? You look like a million dollars."

"Thank you," said Bronwen, smiling. "You don't look too bad yourself. There's something very affecting about bandages."

"I've discovered that," said her brother cheerfully. "They bring out the protective instinct in women."

"Michael," said Bronwen severely, "it's time you stopped ogling and settled down."

"Whatever for?" he asked, grinning.

"Because you're too old to be acting like a silly teenager, that's what for. Although why any woman would put up with you, I can't think."

"There was one once," said Michael unexpectedly.

"Was there?" Bronwen was surprised.

"Mmm. A long time ago."

"And you got cold feet and ran away," she surmised disgustedly.

"Not exactly. She decided to marry someone else."

Bronwen stared at him. There was something in his voice that convinced her that her brother had actually been hurt by that old rejection. Maybe he wasn't quite as thoughtless and superficial as she'd imagined.

But he was changing the subject back to her.

"What's with the fancy jumpsuit, Bron? Is the old shop finally making you a fortune?"

She laughed self-consciously. "No, just an adequate living. Um—Slade bought the jumpsuit."

"Slade!" His eyes narrowed. "What have you been up to, little sister?"

"I haven't been up to anything," she said defensively. "Slade's been very kind, that's all."

"What sort of kind?" asked Michael, frowning with unflattering suspicion.

"Well—he's letting me stay in his suite, and he showed me all around Vancouver." She crumpled a corner of his bedsheet before hurrying on. "He also bought me some clothes because he said I wasn't suitably dressed for the—the weather."

"The weather be damned," said Michael. "Bron, do you have any idea what you're getting into?"

She sighed. "No, not really, but... Is Slade very much of a rake, then, Michael?" She wasn't sure she wanted to hear the answer.

"A rake?" He laughed disbelievingly. "That's hardly the word I'd have used. But, since you ask, in a way I suppose he is. There have always been women panting after him. Lucky devil. But I don't think he cares much for being chased, and whenever there's been anyone—well, semipermanent, I have to admit he's played fair."

"But..." Bronwen choked, and gulped back the words she'd meant to speak. There was no point in bringing up the subject of Jenny Price—with whom Slade *hadn't* played fair. It was just possible that Michael didn't know about Jenny, and it would be unkind to destroy his illusions about his friend.

They switched to less loaded topics, and Slade wasn't mentioned again until Michael murmured obliquely as she was leaving, "Be careful, Bron. My old friend's broken a lot of hearts in his time."

"Well, he won't be breaking mine," said Bronwen, glaring at him.

"Mmm-hmm." He smiled knowingly, and her glare turned into a scowl.

She was still scowling as she stepped off the bus, having firmly refused the taxi driver's offer to pick her up. By the time she reached the lobby of Slade's building she was so disturbed by Michael's hints and insinuations that she didn't notice the small woman watering the plants until she had almost knocked her over.

"Oh, I'm sorry," she gasped, putting out a hand to steady the older woman.

"Never mind, dear." Two birdlike eyes gave her a quick appraisal. "It isn't the only accident I've had today. A parked car hit my bumper a few minutes ago while I was trying to avoid a pedestrian—and this morning my front end was hit by a moving street-light. It came straight at me."

"Oh, dear," said Bronwen faintly. "I'm so sorry. I didn't mean to hit your..." No. No, wait a minute, she *couldn't* apologize for hitting this apparently lethal little lady's front end. "Um..." She began to sidle across to the elevator.

"You're Mr. Slade's new young lady, aren't you?" said the woman, stepping nimbly in front of her, and dashing all hopes of an effective sidle.

"No," said Bronwen. "I'm just a friend. How did you know I'm staying...?"

"Oh, I always know what's going on in this building, dear. I'm Mrs. Bickersley, and I'm known as a *people* person. People, you see, are so much more interesting than *things*."

She beamed at Bronwen, who wondered if her new acquaintance expected a medal for indulging in the universal pastime of minding everyone else's business.

"Umm—that's nice," she muttered uncertainly.

Mrs. Bickersley noticed her discomfort, and the birdlike eyes gleamed. "I expect you're in a hurry, aren't you, dear? Mr. Slade will be waiting for you, will he?"

"Oh, I don't expect so," said Bronwen hastily. She paused with one hand on the elevator button. "Did you say *Mr.* Slade?"

"Yes, naturally, dear. It's his name, isn't it? But perhaps you have a more personal name for the dear man."

"No," said Bronwen quickly. "No, I haven't." She pressed the button and waited for the elevator with her mind going around in circles.

Slade had a name that wasn't Slade. He must have. How extraordinary that it hadn't occurred to her before. But he had always been Slade. Just Slade. Nothing else—even at school, as far as she was aware. She must ask him...

The elevator came, and she slipped in quickly. As the door closed she heard Mrs. Bickersley call after her, "Enjoy yourselves, you carefree young things."

Bronwen winced, and by the time she pushed open the door of Slade's suite she was so angry that she let it crash against the wall.

"Damn the woman," she muttered. "How dare she...?"

Flinging down her bag, she stamped to the counter and picked up a fresh section of wallpaper.

"Good grief!" Slade exclaimed, slamming his briefcase onto the table before peeling off his jacket and slinging it over a chair. "What the hell's going on?" He gestured at the strips of cut paper on the kitchen floor, and the scissors and other weaponry on the counter. "Bronwen, where are you?"

"In here," called Bronwen from the bathroom.

Slade noted that her normally soft voice had a tight edge of temper to it, and he smiled grimly as he strode toward the open door.

Bronwen was perched on a chair, smoothing a sponge doggedly down a strip of wallpaper on which a selection of historic sailing ships ploughed their way across a bright green sea. Her blue jumpsuit was splattered with water and paste.

"And what," asked Slade austerely, "do you think you're doing?"

"Wallpapering." She went on smoothing.

"So I see. May I ask *why* you have chosen to remove the paper I personally selected, in order to replace it with a nursery print?"

Bronwen stumbled on the chair and would have fallen if he hadn't grabbed her by the hips. "Don't you like it?" she asked, steadying herself against the wall and squirming away from his much too stimulating touch. "I thought you would. I looked at your bookshelves and there were all kinds of books about sailing..."

"I happen to enjoy sailing. That doesn't mean I enjoy being redecorated."

"Oh," said Bronwen. She could feel the almost manic energy that had kept her going all day beginning to seep away as she spoke. "I should have thought, I suppose, but I wanted to do something to— to even the score for the clothes——"

"Oh, you evened it all right."

Bronwen forced herself to keep a rein on her temper. "As I was saying—or trying to—the old paper was peeling, and I'd noticed that paint shop around the corner——"

"And you were in a thoroughly bad temper and wanted to work some of it off."

"I suppose so." His voice was terribly stern and disapproving, but there wasn't much point in denying it. The whole of Pontglas had known that when Bronwen Evans was in a temper, which luckily didn't happen often, she blew her allowance on wallpaper and started repapering her room.

"Is there any particular reason why it's upside down?" Slade asked, running his finger lightly down a seam.

The question sounded casual enough, but his voice wasn't quite steady...

"It's not..." she began. Then stopped. "Oh, dear Lord. It is."

And it was. The historic ships over by the window were sailing serenely across a waving green sky.

"You must have been exceptionally put out," remarked Slade equably. "Was it something I said?"

Bronwen looked at him for the first time since he'd entered the bathroom, and it wasn't disapproval she read in the thin curve of his lip or the questioning arch of his eyebrows. It was amusement. Mocking, patronizing amusement. And it was the last straw. She had made a genuine attempt to do him a favor, and all it had done was give him an excuse to mock her. On top of Michael's warnings, Mrs. Bickersley's unveiled insinuations and her own mental confusion, it was just too much.

"Excuse me," she said, jumping to the floor and dashing for the exit with her head down.

Her passage was halted by Slade's arm, which was stretched across the doorway so that she couldn't pass.

"And where do you think you're off to?" he asked conversationally.

"I don't know. Anywhere. Away from here."

"Why? Because I teased you about your wallpaper?"

"No, it's not just that." She stared at the gold-flecked door. "That's only part of it."

"So I assumed. Now tell me what set you off in the first place."

No, she wasn't going to do that. Because *he* had set her off. With his kisses and his teasing, and his beautiful golden body in the morning. The body that could never be hers, because, for all his careless kindness to her, she had reason to know he wasn't a man to trust.

"It was Michael," she said, deciding part of the truth was better than no truth at all. "And that woman. They both think I'm—that you—well, that we..."

"Hold it," said Slade, placing a hand across her mouth to halt further incomprehensible revelations. "I think you had better sit down. Quietly. I'll pour you a drink and then we'll get to the bottom of this nonsense. After which I have a feeling *I'll* be the one in need of refreshment. This is shaping up to be the end of a perfect day."

Bronwen looked up at him doubtfully. He didn't sound bossy or dictatorial any more, but—he was Slade. She saw that his face looked drawn, and there were deep lines of weariness beneath his eyes.

"Have you had a very bad day?" she asked reluctantly.

"You might say so. I had to fire two employees who chose to take advantage of my absence yesterday. Naturally that meant more work for everyone else."

"Did you *have* to sack them?" asked Bronwen. "Couldn't you have given them another chance?"

"No," said Slade, leading her toward the sofa. "I couldn't. We're a rapidly expanding business, and I've no time to waste on incompetents. As a matter of fact, I've replaced them with someone you know."

"But I don't know anyone in Vancouver."

"You've met this one. Remember the bearded delinquent who tried to break into my car? He took me up on that job offer. I think he may work out quite well."

Bronwen shook her head. She'd always known Slade could be ruthless, but she found it hard to reconcile that hard-driving man with this odd, quixotic Slade who turned street kids into respectable business people. He had so many facets to his personality that she was left more or less permanently bewildered.

"Sit down," he ordered, changing the subject abruptly. "I'll join you in a moment. By the way, that blue garment you're wearing does provide *some* compensation for the rigors of my business day. It's very alluring."

"It's not meant to be," said Bronwen quickly as he moved away.

"I was afraid it wasn't." He gave the jumpsuit a brief, unmistakably suggestive appraisal, and disappeared into the kitchen.

Bronwen shook her head. Valerie had said Slade would like this outfit, but she hadn't quite realized . . .

She had no time to finish the thought before he was back, bearing two tall glasses of a drink she hadn't tasted before. Whatever it was, it had the effect of relaxing her.

"Now," said Slade, settling himself in a deep arm-chair and resting an ankle casually over his knee, "let's get this straight. You were mad at me, presumably on general principles, so you started wallpapering——"

"Something like that."

"I thought so. And then you were upset because I wasn't crazy about having my bathroom turned upside down——"

"It isn't all upside down."

"True. Only the bit by the window."

Bronwen stared at him. He was leaning back in the chair with the neck of his shirt unbuttoned and his tie loose, looking as if he hadn't a care in the world. And he was biting his lip as if he was having trouble suppressing a laugh.

She allowed herself a small, tentative smile. "I'm sorry about that," she said, sighing. "I'll change it back—put up more of your green-striped paper."

"But I don't want you to put up more of my green-striped paper. I like your ships."

"You said they were a nursery print."

"So they are. And I don't like carrot-haired maniacs taking over my decorating scheme. On the other hand, I never had a nursery, so it will give me a chance to catch up on my childhood."

Bronwen studied him closely. Was he mocking her or looking for sympathy? Neither, she decided in the end. He was stating a fact and closing a subject that was beginning to bore him.

"I won't redecorate any more," she assured him with considerable feeling.

"No, Miss Evans, you won't. Now—what was that gibberish you were spouting about Michael and some silly woman?"

"Oh." Bronwen shifted uncomfortably. She didn't want to explain, but there was little point in beating about the bush. "Michael thought I shouldn't be staying here," she told him, clasping her hands tightly in her lap. "And I met this funny little woman in the lobby——"

"Oh, heavens," said Slade. "Not Mrs. Bickersley? The people person?"

Bronwen stared at him. "How did you know?"

"Believe me, anyone who has spent more than two days in this building knows all about Mrs. Bickersley. If she can't dig up suitable sex scandals, criminal activity or domestic violence to pin on her fellow residents she soon manages to take it out on their cars."

"Oh-hhh!" exclaimed Bronwen as the light dawned. "She said something about missing a pedestrian, and a parked car hitting her front end. At least, I think that's what she said."

"Probably," agreed Slade. "Not a vintage day for Mrs. B. She usually scores an even half-dozen."

Bronwen put her hand over her mouth, and discovered she was feeling a whole lot better. Until she remembered that Michael too had leaped to conclusions.

"It's not just Mrs. Bickersley, though," she explained, taking a quick sip of her drink. "Michael also disapproves of my being here. I have to move out, Slade."

"What you have to do, my girl, is stop worrying about other people's opinions, including your brother's, and finish your drink. After which I'm taking you out to dinner."

"And if I don't choose to accept your advice?"
Bronwen's eyes were smoky and rebellious.

"Try it and see."

He spoke quite pleasantly, but he looked so cool
and in charge, sprawled there in the big armchair, such
a picture of controlled authority, that she decided she
would put off trying anything for the moment.
Besides, she had already expended most of her spare
energy on the wallpaper—which tomorrow, of course,
would have to be reversed.

In the end he took her out to dinner just as he
planned, and the two of them enjoyed a surprisingly
cordial evening. She supposed that was partly because she was too worn out to argue, and partly because Slade went out of his way to be a charming and
attentive host.

Later, when he brought her home and pushed her
gently in the direction of the bedroom with nothing
more threatening than a brotherly peck on the cheek,
she began to think that, after all, she might actually
grow to like Slade. If only...

But if onlys were futile dreaming, and the past could
never be rewritten.

It was not until she closed the bedroom door that
she remembered something Mrs. Bickersley had said.

"Slade," she said, padding back into the living
room. "What's your name?"

"What?" he was replacing a decanter of whiskey
in the drinks cabinet, and looked at her as though he
doubted her sanity. "Have you been overdoing the
wine, by any chance?"

"No, of course I haven't. It's just that Mrs.
Bickersley—— "

"To hell with Mrs. Bickersley."

"Well, yes," she agreed sweetly. "That may well be her fate. But all the same, she called you *Mr*. Slade."

"I've been called worse things. One of the men I fired today said I was a——"

"Slade, stop it. Do you have a *first* name?"

"Mmm. I'm afraid I do." He closed the cabinet door with a sharp click.

"Well, what is it?"

He sighed. "It's Emlyn. I don't like it. And, if you ever call me anything but Slade, *you* will be responsible for the consequences."

"Which, I suppose, will be swift and unsubtle," Bronwen jeered.

"Definitely. Remember, this is a tall building."

"Does that make a difference?"

"It might. The railing around the balcony is usefully low."

"Really?" said Bronwen interestedly. "I'll *try* to remember. Good night, Emlyn." Grinning impishly, she stepped back into the bedroom and locked the door.

She listened gleefully to the roar of outrage from the other side, and when he said, "Open that door again, young lady, and I promise you *you* won't have a good night," she burst out laughing.

There was a speculative look in Slade's eye when she rose dutifully in the morning to make his breakfast. It was as though he hadn't quite made up his mind what to do about her.

Eventually he confirmed her suspicion when she remarked that it was a great shame he had to work today.

"I don't have to," he said shortly. "However, it's our busiest day and I prefer to keep an eye on things—

when it's convenient. Which, in fact, it may not be today. I haven't decided whether to deal with you now or later.''

"Deal with me?" she asked, feigning bewilderment.

"Mmm. I told you you wouldn't like the consequences if you called me anything but Slade."

"Oh," said Bronwen, unperturbed. "You'd better make it later, then. If you throw me off the balcony now you'll have to make your own breakfast."

"A very good point," he agreed soberly. "I'll have to rethink the situation. At least until Mrs. Doyle returns."

"What a relief," murmured Bronwen, placing a plate of eggs before him and flouncing away.

"You," he said, catching her wrist as she moved off, and pulling her up hard against his knee, "could do with a damn good shaking."

"What a violent man you are," she gibed, twisting free and spinning back into the kitchen. "Mrs. Bickersley would be delighted if she could hear you."

"Mrs. Bickersley won't be the recipient," replied Slade grimly.

Bronwen didn't answer, and when he left about twenty minutes later, after kissing her unexpectedly on the lips, she still wasn't quite sure if he was amused, or if he really did mean to exact some form of penalty on his return.

She spent the rest of the morning washing Slade's piles of clothes, tidying the suite, removing the upside-down wallpaper and replacing it with a new panel, and gazing out of the large window at the stunning view of the inlet and the mountains. They were clear at first, then covered with a faint, smoky haze. Later, when she went outside, she noticed that the air had become hot, heavy and oppressive.

By the time she returned from her sisterly visit to Michael, Slade was already in the suite and the mountains had a brooding look about them.

The first clap of thunder came just as she put down her bag.

"Don't you like thunder?" asked Slade when he saw her jump. He was sprawled in the armchair again, looking irritatingly at ease in casual gray pants and a blue shirt.

"I don't mind it," she replied. "I was startled, that's all." She glanced at the window and added doubtfully, "It seems to be getting very dark."

"Yes, I imagine we're in for a storm."

Bronwen could have kicked him for sounding so unconcerned about it. She didn't care about the storm, but the room was becoming so very *dark*.

"I'll put some lights on," said Slade after a brief, perceptive look at her face.

He didn't suggest they go out this evening, for which she was grateful. Without being asked, she went into the kitchen to heat up another of Mrs. Doyle's creations. She was even glad that, true to form, Slade didn't offer to help her. It was a relief to have something to do as the sound of thunder rumbled closer and a pale yellow twilight cast long shadows into the room.

They ate more or less in silence, and afterward Bronwen couldn't recall what she'd served up. She was too conscious of a threat that for once didn't emanate from Slade. He was aware of her discomfort, she knew, because he kept glancing at her and then looking away with a quick frown.

As soon as they had finished he got up and drew the soft gray-patterned draperies across the windows.

"Why did you do that?" asked Bronwen. "You never draw your curtains."

"I do when my companion is so jittery that she forgets to make coffee for me."

That roused her from her unreasonable anxiety. "Your turn," she said. "I made dinner."

"Actually, Mrs. Doyle did."

"Even so——"

"Even so, you've decided to dig your toes in. But you'll be much happier if you keep occupied, won't you?" He sat down again, crossed his arms, and smiled with infuriating smugness.

Bronwen knew he was right about her need to keep busy, and after delivering a glare that would have demolished a lesser man than Slade she got up to put on the coffee.

When she came back he had turned on all the lights in the apartment, and the cool room seemed much warmer than usual—until somewhere around nine o'clock, when a clap of thunder sounded right above their heads.

Five minutes after that lightning sizzled on the other side of the curtains, and every light in the building went out.

Bronwen gave a little moan of distress, and Slade moved unerringly into the kitchen and came back, carrying a flashlight.

"Right," he said, coming purposefully around the table to stand beside her. "That will be quite enough of that. Come on, you're going straight to bed, where you can pull the covers up around your ears and pretend it's just any ordinary night. That's what you usually do, isn't it? And, if past experience is anything to go by, it'll be several hours before the power comes back."

"I'm all right," insisted Bronwen, clinging to the table with both hands.

"You are not all right. You're scared stiff."

"No, really..."

"Bronwen," he said, keeping his voice down with some difficulty, "stop arguing. I'm in no mood to put up with false heroics. Especially when they're so *obviously* false. I know all about Michael's little prank when you were a kid. Remind me to scalp him for it when he's better. But in the meantime we'll concentrate on you. You're going to bed, where you'll feel safe and warm, and where the dark won't matter any more." He caught her wrists and pulled her onto her feet. "Go on."

"No, I——"

"I said, get going."

"Slade, stop bullying me. I tell you, I'm fine."

"And I tell you you're not fine. What's more, if you don't get moving this minute I'll do more than bully you. I'll undress you and put you to bed myself."

She stole a worried glance at him through her lashes, and saw something in the thin line of his lips that convinced her he meant what he said. She gulped, not sure now which was the greater threat—Slade, or the dark.

When he put out a hand and unfastened the top button of her blouse with a businesslike flick of his fingers her mind was very speedily made up.

"I'm going," she said quickly. "Keep your hands off me."

"Certainly. I'll come and tuck you in."

"I'm not a child, and you're not my father," she snapped, stumbling for the bedroom as another peal of thunder shook the building.

"You're certainly right on the latter point," muttered Slade. "Here, take the flashlight." He came up behind her and put it into her hand.

"What about you?" she whispered.

"I can see in the dark," he replied dryly.

She wouldn't put it past him, she thought as exasperation temporarily overcame her anxiety. There *was* something catlike about him.

Taking the flashlight without speaking, she hurried into the bedroom, tore off her clothes and made a frantic dive for the bed.

She took Slade's advice and buried her head beneath the covers, and it was only as she began to relax in her cocoon that it came to her that she'd neglected to put on her nightgown. Slade would approve. Not that it mattered, because Slade wasn't going to find out. Strange how he had seemed to know that she always hid in bed on those rare occasions when she had to cope with unexpected darkness. Perhaps Michael had told him...

Another flash of lightning zinged through a crack in the curtains, and she poked her head up. The room was dark as black ink. Funny, darkness had never prevented her from falling asleep, and she had long ago outgrown a night-light. Perhaps it was the idea that she *couldn't* flood the room with light if she had to that frightened her most...

She groped for the flashlight, couldn't find it, and unwittingly gave a low cry of alarm.

Slade was standing at the big window with his hands thrust into his pockets. The curtains were thrown open to the night. He flung his head back, exulting in the play of light and dark across the inlet, reveling in the wildness of the storm, and the dangerous fingers of gold forking their way down the sky. His lips drew back from his teeth in a grin of pure exhilaration.

At that moment he heard Bronwen's cry.

He stiffened and turned to listen. Yes, there it was again. With a regretful glance at the elements warring so spectacularly outside he strode briskly to the bedroom door and knocked.

"Bronwen," he said sharply. "What is it?"

"Nothing." Her voice was muffled.

"Are you still afraid?"

"No-o."

Oh, sure, thought Slade in exasperation, hearing the unmistakable quiver in her voice. The way a cornered mouse isn't scared of a cat. "Bronwen," he said quietly, "open the door."

"It's locked."

"It would be. Never mind, hang on."

Bronwen was hanging on. To the bedpost. When the next flash of lightning lighted the room she saw that the handle was turning, and then Slade was inside, coming toward her—sitting down on the edge of the bed . . .

"I'm all right. Really," she said, as much to convince herself as him.

"So I see," he replied, patiently removing her clenched fingers from the bedpost and holding both her hands in his own. "Bronwen, there's no need to panic. You're quite safe."

"Yes, I know," she whispered. "I'm sorry. It's not the storm, it's the dark. I couldn't find the torch."

"It's right here." He pulled it off the bedside table and turned it on. "Did you know it's called a flashlight on this continent?"

"Is it?" She didn't care what it was called as long as it worked.

He regarded the exposed skin between her neck and the top of the covers with a slight frown. "You'll be fine now," he said, dropping her hands abruptly. "Get some sleep."

"Slade, please——"

"What's the matter?"

His voice was rough, not patient, as it had sounded before. It was as though he was anxious to get away from her. But she didn't want him to go away. Surprisingly she wasn't afraid any more, and it had nothing to do with the flashlight. It was Slade who made her feel safe, sitting here beside her—on her bed. No, it was *his* bed, wasn't it? And she wasn't wearing any clothes. She ran a hand over her forehead, taking care not to disarrange the covers. Was she going crazy? How could she possibly feel safe with Slade, of all people?

He stood up, headed for the door, and she knew that, whether it made sense or not, she couldn't bear it if he went away.

"Don't go," she whispered. "Please don't go."

He stopped with his hand on the doorframe. "Do you have any idea what you're asking?" he demanded, still with his back to her.

"I . . ." She hesitated. "I'm asking you to stay. To keep me company, Slade. You—you make me feel safe."

"Safe!" he exclaimed, spinning around and leaning against the doorframe, so that she could see the shadows playing across his features as a flash from the window set his bright hair on fire. "Bronwen, for heaven's sake, in case you haven't noticed, I'm a man, and, unless I'm very much mistaken, you're naked. Even if you aren't, there's only one bed in this room.

Or perhaps you imagine I'm going to sleep on the floor."

"I—I *had* noticed you're a man," she murmured.

He swore, briefly, competently, and in the sort of voice that left her in no doubt that he meant every word. When he stopped she said, "I'm sorry. I didn't mean——"

"What *did* you mean, Bronwen?" he asked harshly. "That I'm to spend the night in your bed keeping you *company*?" He poured a wealth of scorn into the word. "Don't you realize...?"

Quite suddenly Bronwen did realize. She was asking this virile, masterful man to spend the night with her— because she was scared and he gave her comfort. But if he heeded her request she might have a lot more than the dark to be afraid of. Only—the strange thing was, she wasn't afraid at all. Quite the contrary.

Lightning flared again, and she stared into the afterglow and said slowly, "Slade, I don't want you to leave me. Please stay."

CHAPTER SIX

FOR a moment Slade didn't say a word, but stood like sculpted stone against the door. Then he uttered one brief, very succinct phrase and strode across to the bed.

Bronwen held out her hands, and he took them and sat down beside her.

"Bronwen," he said huskily, "don't you know you're asking for trouble? Or are you too damned innocent to recognize trouble when you see it?"

"Not when it comes with long legs, blue eyes and a smile any girl would kill for," she said softly. "I recognize that kind of trouble."

"Then why...?"

"I told you. You make me feel safe."

He groaned and pressed both fists into the covers beside her shoulders. Their eyes met, dark and mysterious in the shadowy light, and gradually Slade relaxed his arms and touched his mouth to her lips.

It wasn't the kiss she expected. Neither reluctant, nor let's-get-on-with-it impatient. Instead it was warm, drugging, gently exploratory, as if it was the beginning of something wonderful that would last forever.

In fact, it lasted about thirty seconds before Slade groaned again and lifted his head.

"Good night, Bronwen," he said, beginning to rise.

"No." She put out her hand and caught him by the wrist. "Don't go."

"If I don't go," he said in a clipped, almost angry voice, "both of us are likely to regret it."

She knew what he meant, but somehow the danger wasn't real. All that *was* real was Slade's comforting presence, his tall body looming above her in the shadows—and the darkness that would overwhelm her if he left.

"Hold me," she whispered. "Please, Slade. Just for a minute."

"I'm not made of ice," he rasped. "You're asking too much of me, Bronwen."

"Too much? Because I asked you to hold me?"

Slade picked up the flashlight, pointed it at her face and saw the big gray eyes fixed on him, wide and imploring. He shook his head in growing disbelief. Surely no modern young woman was *that* innocent? Not when she was lying there with no clothes on. She *couldn't* expect him to play the part of a eunuch. Could she? He deliberated a moment before reaching the only possible conclusion. No twenty-six-year-old woman could be that guileless. His shy little village girl wasn't as inexperienced as he'd thought.

He frowned, and his lips compressed into a flat line that Bronwen couldn't see. Then he sank down onto the bed and, with businesslike purpose, pulled her up into his arms. The sheet was still tucked discreetly around her neck.

She felt him stiffen as her breasts hardened against his chest. A feeling of languorous warmth invaded her—a warmth that gradually became an insistent, pulsing need. She wrestled her arms from the sheet and looped them behind his neck, resting her cheek on his shoulder.

At once Slade put his hands up to loosen her grip. He held her away from him, glaring into her eyes as another flash of lightning lighted the room.

"I made you a promise," he growled.

"What promise?" She was genuinely bewildered.

"That I'd keep my hands off you. I know I haven't altogether kept my side of the bargain, but I'm beginning to think that might be because you didn't want it kept."

"I did . . ."

"Did you? And now? I'm not just a convenient refuge from the dark, Bronwen. But I think you know that."

Yes, she knew that. Yet in this dreamlike space which seemed to have no past or future the only thing that mattered was that Slade was here, with her, not being cool and sarcastic any longer, but kind in a gruff sort of way. And he smelled wonderful. Spicy and seductive. Smiling, she lifted her arms again and linked them back around his neck.

The sheet slipped down to her waist.

Slade muttered something under his breath and pushed her roughly back on the pillows. She could feel the buttons of his shirt pressing into her skin as he fell on top of her, and without thinking about it at all she began to unfasten the top one.

"You haven't had much practice at this, have you?" he murmured against her cheek a minute later, when the button remained obdurately in place.

"Not much," she whispered.

"But enough." His voice had a strained, harsh edge to it.

Bronwen didn't contradict him, and a little later the shirt tumbled softly to the floor. She ran her hands tentatively down his back, smoothed them over the tight fabric across his hips, and with a sound that was a cross between a laugh and something unprintable Slade drew her fingers to his belt.

His pants followed the shirt to the floor.

"You feel just the way I thought you would," she whispered, continuing her delicious explorations.

"And how was that?" There was laughter in the question, and his lips began a gentle assault on parts of her that she had never known were meant to be kissed.

"Firm, tough, but smooth in all the right places..."

"What places?" Amusement still quivered beneath the surface.

She laughed mischievously, and showed him. He gave a strangled gasp. "My goodness," he said in a strangled voice. "And I thought..." He broke off abruptly to silence her teasing laughter with his lips.

"Slade," she said breathlessly when he raised his head. "Slade, please, I want——"

"I know." His mouth closed over hers again, and she felt his thigh press between her legs. "So do I, Bronwen. Dear heaven, so do I."

The thunder seemed far away now, drowned out by the beating of her heart. Or was it his heart? She didn't know, didn't care. All that was important was that Slade didn't stop the wonderful things he was doing to her, that whatever was happening would go on happening.

But Slade did stop. "Bronwen," he said, propping himself on one elbow, "Bronwen, do you know what you're doing? Are you sure?"

She wasn't sure of anything, but she nodded anyway, because she knew that what she had started must be finished. She wouldn't be able to bear it if it wasn't.

The thunder rumbled distantly in the mountains, and it wasn't lightning that suddenly illuminated her world. The flash of gold that lighted the sky was Slade—and, even as she bit back a cry of surprisingly sweet pain, she knew that for her the earth could never be the same again. Now and forever it would be colored by the knowledge of love.

"Bronwen?" It was only a few minutes later, but the room was very dark because the flashlight had abruptly given out. "Bronwen, what in *hell* . . . ?"

He was lying still and unnaturally rigid beside her, so she put out her hand and touched it to his cheek. He flinched and drew away from her caress.

"What's the matter?" she asked, puzzled. She felt happy, at peace, totally unafraid, even though the room was in darkness. Slade's lovemaking had finally banished the dark. She had a feeling it was banished forever.

But it was apparent he didn't feel the same.

"You little idiot," he said savagely. "Why didn't you tell me?"

"Tell you what?"

"That I was the first. Hell, Bronwen, do you think for a moment I'd have touched you if I'd known?"

Looking back on it, Bronwen had a sense that she'd known very well he wouldn't touch her. But she had wanted him to . . .

"No," she said in a small voice, staring at the faint outline of his profile. "No, I didn't think that."

"Then what——?"

"I *wanted* you to touch me," she said simply.

Slade swore.

"There's no need for that," she told him, a little sharply.

"There is."

"Oh. Didn't—wasn't I . . . ?"

"You were wonderful. Unbelievably wonderful." He was silent for a moment, then turned on his side and ran his fingers absently through her hair.

She smiled in the darkness. "So why——?"

"Bronwen." He sounded exasperated. "Bronwen, until a few minutes ago you were a sweet, maddening, and, I suspect, exceedingly *stupid* virgin. If I'd realized——" He broke off. "Didn't anyone ever tell you how babies are made?"

His scornful impatience made her wince. "Yes," she said, with a surge of bitter remembrance. "Now that you mention it, Jenny Price told me, for one."

The sound of Slade's indrawn breath hissed through the still air of the bedroom, and she saw his fingers flex against the sheet.

"Of course," he said bleakly. "For a moment I forgot."

Bronwen had forgotten too. For those brief, wonderful moments, because of the darkness and Slade's closeness and—she had to admit it—because of her own deep, hitherto unacknowledged hunger, the past had been conveniently dead.

But it wasn't dead any longer. And Slade was right about one thing. She *had* been incredibly stupid. She had practically invited him into her bed and she had taken no precautions whatsoever. It had never occurred to her that she might need them. And, to be fair, it was only natural that he had assumed she knew what she was getting into. He had *asked* her if she knew what she was doing.

And now, Bronwen Evans, she said to herself grimly, you're on your own.

"It's all right," she said to the man lying stiffly beside her. "You needn't worry. I wouldn't hold you responsible."

"Maybe not, Michael's sister, but I would."

She was about to reply, when there was a flicker of light beneath the doorway. Slade eased his feet to the floor, stood up, and pulled on his pants. "The power's on," he said shortly, flicking the switch and filling the room with light.

Bronwen blinked. "Yes," she agreed. "I'll be all right now, thank you, Slade."

"Spoken like a true duchess," he gibed. "But, as I'm not your servant to be dismissed once the job's completed, I don't plan on leaving until I'm ready."

She moved her head on the pillow. What on earth was happening to her and Slade? A little while ago they had been lovers. Now they were behaving like two people who heartily disliked one another. But she didn't dislike him. Not any more. Not even when she thought of Jenny Price. She gave a soft, unintentional moan, and closed her eyes. She knew what that meant. If she could forgive Slade for Jenny she could forgive him anything. Because she loved him. Perhaps, without knowing it, she always had.

She opened her eyes and saw that his blue gaze was fixed on her with steady inflexibility.

"We'll get married as soon as possible," he said flatly, snapping closed the buckle on his belt.

Bronwen gaped at him. "We'll what?"

"Get married as soon as possible." He picked up his shirt and slung it over his shoulder. "I'll see to the details tomorrow. In the meantime we'll stick to our old sleeping arrangements, shall we? Since I gather I've served my purpose for tonight."

"I—I..." She opened her mouth, closed it, and swallowed. "Slade," she at last managed to gasp out, "Slade, you're being ridiculous. Of course I don't expect you to marry me."

"Maybe not. But I'm going to, just the same."

"You are not!" She struggled up, clasping the sheet across her chest. "I—I don't want to marry you."

"That's too bad, isn't it?" He turned his back on her and reached for the handle of the door.

Bronwen finally gave in to the urge she'd been suppressing ever since she'd met up again with Slade. With a quick movement she picked up the nearest pillow and aimed it deliberately at his head.

It hit him with a satisfying thud.

"Feel better?" he asked, turning on his heel and raising an unbelievably nonchalant eyebrow. He bent down, collected the pillow and tossed it carelessly back onto the bed. Either by accident or design, it landed smack across her face.

By the time she had extricated herself from the returning missile Slade had gone.

"Damn him," she muttered, reaching behind her for her sensible white nightdress. She pulled it on, frowning.

At Slade's insistence, she had purchased two slinky silk garments from Valerie, but she hadn't yet had the nerve to wear one. They weren't her style somehow. The white museum piece was, and tonight it gave her comfort, like an old friend. She needed comfort, because the big bed had become enormous and very lonely.

Lying back against the pillows, she closed her eyes, wishing the old confusion would return. The trouble was, she wasn't confused any longer. She knew exactly what had happened. She had fallen in love with Slade, in spite of her conviction that he was an impossible kind of man to love. That was why she had done something so out of character as to move in with a man whose morals she didn't trust. It was also why tonight they had been lovers. It had nothing much to do with her fear of the dark, and everything to do with the way she felt about Slade. And it *had* been like nothing she'd ever dreamed of...

But, of course, he didn't love her. She knew that with a sort of weary despair. He had informed her, briskly, that they were getting married, but that had to be because he was suffering from an attack of conscience.

She shifted her head restlessly. It was strange in a way. He had shown no conscience over Jenny, who was the mother of his child. Bronwen frowned. Perhaps it wasn't so strange after all. He had called her "Michael's sister" again, and it was quite possible that he felt a loyalty to his friend that he was incapable of feeling toward a woman he had loved lightly once, and left.

Not that any of it really mattered, she decided bleakly. Because there was no way in the world she would marry Slade. She didn't believe in marrying without love—and, although on his side there might be a certain affection, there was no question of anything more. If she accepted his casually autocratic proposal she would only be asking for heartbreak.

She closed her eyes, willing herself to sleep. There was nothing to be gained by all this soul-searching.

It was nearly morning by the time she finally drifted off—only to dream of Slade's arms around her, the cool male scent of his body—and the touch of his firm lips on her own...

When she woke the sky was bright blue outside her window and Slade was nowhere in sight. Or sound, she realized as she pulled on her robe and called his name. After a brief search of the suite she was forced to the conclusion that he'd left. She looked at her watch—11:00 a.m. He was at work, of course.

After a while she peered into the kitchen sink and spied an unappealing array of dirty dishes, sprinkled with flecks of burnt toast. She smiled grimly. A night of passion and provocation had obviously done nothing to improve Slade's cooking. But at least he'd been considerate enough to let her sleep.

The elevator door clanged, she turned off the tap, and immediately the room was filled with Slade. It was amazing how much smaller it seemed when he was in it.

"Hello," she said, feeling inexplicably shy all of a sudden.

He nodded at her. "Hi. It's all settled."

"What is?" she asked, with an uncomfortable feeling that she already knew the answer.

"The wedding. I've arranged it for Friday."

Bronwen stopped feeling shy. "I'm not marrying you, Slade," she said through teeth she was trying hard not to grind.

He removed his imposing dark jacket and flung it over a chair. "So you said last night. But, if you'll stop to think it over, it's the only sensible solution."

"I have thought it over, and I see nothing remotely sensible about it."

Slade loosened his tie. "You should. There are certain obvious advantages."

"Such as?" She put her hands on her hips and glared at him but it was difficult to feel belligerent when he was standing there, smiling in a way that was both sexy and implacable, and looking as if he was undressing her with his eyes.

"Well," he drawled, "bed, for instance. I don't know about you, but I found it exceptionally satisfactory."

He did know about her, she thought indignantly. He knew she'd found it *more* than satisfactory. "There's a lot more to marriage than that," she informed him loftily.

"Mmm. So I've been told. I can't wait to find out for myself."

"Well, you'll have to wait," Bronwen told him.

"Yes. Until Friday."

This time she did grind her teeth. "Slade, what do I have to do to convince you? I wouldn't marry you if—if..."

"If I were the last man left in the world? Is that the somewhat hackneyed phrase you had in mind? Why not, Bronwen? You didn't object to my company last night."

"That was different."

"Was it? You're the love 'em and leave 'em type, are you?"

"No," she snapped. "No, Slade, *I'm* not."

"Ah," he said, moving across to the window. "I'm beginning to see. You think I am, don't you?"

"How can I think anything else? What about Jenny? You left her."

His mouth suddenly reminded her of a steel trap. "Did I?"

"Of course you did. And you didn't ask *her* to marry you."

"No," he said flatly. "Because I didn't want to marry Jenny Price any more than she wanted to marry me. However, I do want to marry you, my dear."

"Why? You don't love me."

"Don't I?" His voice was as forbidding as his face, and, watching it, Bronwen couldn't believe he would ask that question.

"Of course you don't," she said—even as a lump formed in her throat and she wished with all her heart it weren't true.

"Would it help you to get over your scruples if I said I did love you?" he asked, flicking a speck of dust from his sleeve.

"No." She sighed. "I wouldn't believe you."

"I didn't think you would. In that case, I'll save my breath. Now, about Friday . . ."

Bronwen gave up. There was no point in arguing with him in this mood. When his mind was made up he was like a machete, slashing a path through the jungle. Except that he didn't even acknowledge the jungle's existence. He'd always been like that, though, she remembered—and the only thing she could do now was pretend to go along with him and make her own plans quietly on the side.

She listened meekly as he told her the church he'd chosen, the minister he'd asked to perform the ceremony, and explained to her that there wouldn't be time to organize a large reception, but that they would have one when they returned from their honeymoon.

"Honeymoon?" said Bronwen faintly.

"Mmm. Greece, I think, don't you?"

She nodded blankly. He could suggest Mars or Venus, for all she cared, because she wasn't going anywhere with Slade.

"I have to get back to work," he said. "We'll go over any further details this evening. Let me know if you think of anything I've forgotten."

Bronwen didn't reply, and his eyes narrowed. "You're very quiet all of a sudden," he remarked.

"You've taken my breath away," she replied truthfully.

He smiled. "Good. You're much less trouble when you're not breathing." He stepped toward her, put one arm around her waist and kissed her possessively on the mouth. To her utter dismay, she found herself returning his embrace.

"Be good while I'm gone," he said, flicking her lightly on the cheek. Then he picked up his jacket and tie and walked out of the door, whistling a tuneless little air between his teeth.

Bronwen wandered back into the bedroom, and with almost robotlike efficiency began to make up the bed. After that, and still moving automatically, she put on the green skirt and sweater she'd arrived in, all the while staring hopelessly around the room where she had known such unexpected joy. Her gaze lighted on the battered suitcases that she had relegated to a corner by the window.

Half an hour later the suitcases were neatly packed, but only with the clothes she'd brought with her. For a moment she stared wistfully at the cream-and-gold creation Slade had admired so, but after a slight hesitation she closed the cupboard door firmly and went to make a last quick check of the apartment.

Slade's dishes still lay forlornly in the sink.

She paused, made an effort to ignore them, and in the end decided she couldn't stand it. In any case, washing his dirty dishes might be the last thing she ever did for Slade.

By the time she had emptied the water it was mixed with the salt of the tears that she could no longer hold back. Life with Slade might be impossible, but life without him would be as bleak and dry as the desert.

Dashing a hand across her eyes, she lifted her chin and straightened her shoulders defiantly. No, it would *not* be bleak and dry. She'd been happy before she'd left Wales and she would be again. No blond Viking of a man with a smile like a seductive magnet was going to make *her* unhappy for long. She wouldn't allow it.

As she picked up her suitcases and pulled the door to behind her Bronwen refused to look back—until the elevator slid open at the bottom floor. And by that time it was already too late.

Mrs. Bickersley was standing in the lobby, waving her watering can over a scuffed spot on the carpet.

"Ah, my dear," she chirruped. "I've been thinking about you."

Bronwen groaned inwardly. "Are you watering the floor, Mrs. Bickersley?" she asked with an acidity she usually reserved for shoplifters and customers who didn't pay their bills.

"What? Oh, no, my dear, I came down to water the plants," replied Slade's maddening neighbor with a virtuous smile.

"Maintenance took the plants away yesterday," Bronwen reminded her dryly.

"Did they, dear? I really hadn't noticed. Imagine that, now."

Bronwen could well imagine it. The building's resident minder of the other people's business hadn't yet thought of a reason as convenient as the plants for taking up her station in the lobby.

"Are you leaving, dear?" she asked as Bronwen lugged her cases to the door.

She resisted the urge to say, "What does it look like?" and answered with a brief, "Yes."

"Really? Oh, dear, Mr. Slade will be disappointed. Does he know?"

If he didn't he soon would, Bronwen thought—and long before he read the note she'd left him.

"I expect so," she replied evasively.

Mrs. Bickersley's bird eyes brightened. "You've had a falling out, haven't you?" she said archly. "I can tell because I'm such a people person. I used to counsel troubled souls as a volunteer, you know. But they told me they didn't need me after one of the paid staff tried to kill me. So unfair, because he kept *his* job, and I heard he'd even been given a promotion." She sighed. "I enjoyed that job."

"Oh," said Bronwen. "I'm sorry." At any other time she would have had trouble controlling her laughter. Today all she longed for was escape. She turned quickly toward the heavy glass doors.

"You haven't answered me, dear." The people person didn't give up easily. "You *have* had a falling out, haven't you?"

"Yes," said Bronwen shortly. "Goodbye, Mrs. Bickersley."

"Oh, but..."

Bronwen didn't hear the rest, because she was busy shuffling her cases through the door. When she glanced back and saw that her interrogator was about to follow her outside she started to run lopsidedly for the bus.

As it turned out, the bus was heading downtown, and she got off in the heart of the hotel district. Slade had convinced her that it wouldn't be advisable for her to return to the man-eating sunflowers. Nor was Michael's apartment likely to prove much better.

She sighed. Good hotels were expensive, but she had no choice.

In the end she found a smallish one on Robson Street that didn't look too intimidating, and arranged to stay there for the night while she made up her mind what to do next.

She was lying in the bath, staring gloomily at a large suitcase bruise on her knee, when she heard the phone ring. She ignored it. No one knew she was here, so it had to be a wrong number. It rang twice more. Not a caller who admits his mistakes easily, she thought with a feeling of exasperation. She was in no mood for conversation. It was difficult enough trying to make a decision when you felt as if nothing mattered any more. A noisy telephone was an almost intolerable interruption.

The ringing ceased abruptly. Fifteen minutes later, as she was slipping into her blue shirtwaister it was followed by a peremptory knock on the door.

"Who is it?" she called wearily.

"Your jilted bridegroom," replied a tightly controlled voice from the hallway. "Open up at once or I'll do it for you."

CHAPTER SEVEN

BRONWEN closed her eyes. "What do you want?" she asked rudely.

"You, among other things. I said, open up."

"No."

"Bronwen, the hotel might take a dim view of it if I break the door down, but I promise you that isn't going to stop me."

No, she supposed it wouldn't. Nothing ever stopped Slade once he was set on a specific course of action. But even *he* couldn't marry a woman who refused to say the words "I do."

Smoothing her damp hair back, she walked slowly across to the door. There was no point in calling the desk for help. Even if he was taken away in handcuffs, Slade would find some way to get what he wanted.

"For the last time, are you going to let me in?" he demanded in a voice that meant immediate business.

She opened the door. "Do you always have to have your own way?" she asked, feigning a bored indifference she didn't feel.

"Invariably." He stepped across the threshold, took her by the shoulders, and pulled her up against his chest. "And do you always have to be so much damn trouble? I've got better things to do than chase halfway across the city after you." There was a steely note in his voice, and the glint in his eyes held about as much warmth as winter on the moon.

Involuntarily she shivered, but when his fingers began to tighten on her shoulders she tossed her head and said bitingly, "Why don't you do them, then? I didn't *ask* you to chase after me, Slade." She frowned as something else occurred to her. "How did you find out I was here?"

"Mrs. Bickersley," he said tersely.

She shrugged herself free of his grasp. "Oh. But she didn't know——"

"Oh, yes, she did. Once our neighborhood people hound has her nose set on a scent she doesn't give up until she has her quarry cornered. You piqued her curiosity, my sweet. She followed you. Which saved me a great deal of time."

"But how did she...?"

"I've no idea. Nor do I particularly care, in view of the fact that she managed to score a bull's-eye on my rear bumper in her haste to pass on the good news. Another bone I have to pick with you, Miss Evans."

"I'm sorry about your bumper. But as to the rest——"

"As to the rest, you're coming straight back to my apartment with me, and if you're very lucky I may refrain from wrapping you in the remains of your damn wallpaper and shipping you home to Pontglas."

"I can think of worse fates," said Bronwen dryly.

"So can I. Don't tempt me."

"Slade, I *can't* go back with you. I'm not going to marry you, and——"

"I see. I'm one of those 'worse fates you can think of,' I suppose." The look he gave her was hard and unusually daunting.

"No. Yes. I don't know..."

"Make up your mind."

"It is made up. I'm not marrying you. Just this once, you're not getting your own way."

"We'll see. In the meantime you *are* coming home with me. I had a call from Michael when he found he couldn't reach you. He's been released from the hospital, and I've already installed him at my place to convalesce. He needs you to look after him, Bronwen—which I understand is why you came to Vancouver." The blue eyes beamed a cool assurance that this was an argument he knew he couldn't lose.

He didn't.

"All right," she agreed tiredly. "For Michael's sake, you win."

"I generally do," he remarked, so matter-of-factly that she had a feeling he was merely stating the truth.

They drove back to Slade's apartment in silence. Bronwen felt like a truant being summarily returned to school. What Slade felt, she wasn't sure, but, from the crooked tilt to his mouth, she hadn't much doubt that it was partly smug satisfaction—which did nothing to improve her frame of mind.

They found Michael stretched out on the sea green sofa, impersonating a wounded hero. When Bronwen stepped toward him he gave her a stoical smile. "I've been let out of jail," he informed her, not sounding particularly delighted.

"My sympathies," she replied, touching a hand lightly to his forehead.

"What?" He looked startled.

"No more attractive acolytes to tend your needs," she explained with a sisterly smile.

He grinned. "Never mind, you'll do instead—at least until I'm back on my feet."

Behind her, Slade made a sound that was probably a snort. "Best of luck," he said cryptically.

Bronwen swung around. "You haven't done so badly by me," she snapped. "I've cooked your meals, done your laundry, and..." She stopped abruptly as she saw his eyebrows slant up an unlikely angle.

"Yes?" he said, with a wealth of meaning. "*And...?*"

Michael cleared his throat disapprovingly. Bron's my sister," he said, obviously trying to sound patriarchal, but not succeeding. "Slade, if you've..."

"I haven't," said Slade. "As a matter of fact, I want to marry your sister. I've an idea that's why she ran away. It's hardly flattering."

Michael choked. "*You* actually want to get married!" he exclaimed, running a hand wildly through his hair. "To Bron? Are you serious, Slade, or——?"

"Oh, yes, I'm serious. But, if you suspect I'm suffering from the effects of too much unexpected sun, I have to agree it seems likely."

"If you two have *quite* finished talking about me," said Bronwen, "perhaps we can get down to business."

Slade put his hands in the pockets of his light gray pants and propped himself against the wall next to the door. "I presume that suggestion isn't as promising as it sounds," he said dryly. "What business did you have in mind, my dear?"

She took a deep breath. "Sleeping arrangements," she replied, fixing her gaze on a green floor tile that seemed a shade darker than the others.

"Well," began Slade, "Michael assures me he's very comfortable on the sofa, which leaves——"

"No," said Bronwen, lowering herself into the closest chair.

Michael stared at her. "Bron, I suppose if you and Slade are getting married..." he began hesitantly.

"Slade and I are not," said Bronwen, enunciating each word very clearly, "getting married."

"Oh, yes, we are," he contradicted her smoothly. "But, since you insist on complicating the issue, I will bow to your maidenly misgivings and take up temporary lodgings with Mrs. Bickersley. Will that suit you?" He stared blandly up at the ceiling.

"Don't be idiotic," retorted Bronwen, who hadn't cared for the cynical way his lips had lifted when he referred to her misgivings as "maidenly."

Slade grinned irritatingly. "All right, if that idea doesn't grab you, how about if I move to my country residence—until we're married, of course?"

"You don't have a country residence."

"He does, you know," interrupted Michael. "Ten acres out near Alouette Lake—with a fifteen room ranch-style place to match. And a swimming pool."

Bronwen clenched her fingers on the chair arm and glowered up at Slade suspiciously. "You never mentioned it."

"Didn't I? Perhaps I didn't think you'd be interested."

"Of course I would. I could have stayed there——"

"Safe from the big bad wolf? But think how dull that would have been. And not in the least convenient."

"For me or for you?" she demanded, not giving up.

"For both of us, I should think. Quite apart from other considerations, and although it may have escaped your notice, I'm not a chartered taxi service, Miss Evans."

"Meaning?"

"Meaning it's a long way between my house and the hospital. Or were you expecting a limousine?"

"No, of course not."

He shrugged. "I could have provided one, of course, but I saw no point."

You wouldn't have, thought Bronwen. But she didn't say it.

Slade seemed to consider the subject closed, and when he continued to regard her sleepily from beneath half-closed eyes she found herself asking reluctantly, "If getting to your house and back is such a problem, why are you offering to move there?"

"Because," he said, shifting his shoulders, "it strikes me that, if I don't, by the time our wedding day rolls around I will probably have murdered my blushing bride. Or at the very least indulged in some forgivably therapeutic violence."

"Violence is never forgivable," said Bronwen piously. "Not that I need to worry about it, because we aren't going to have a wedding day."

"So you keep saying. I'm getting rather tired of it," drawled Slade, settling himself against the wall as if he meant to spend the evening holding it up.

Michael, whose bright gaze had been shifting between them with increasing interest, said suddenly, "You might as well give in, Bron, because Slade won't."

Slade inclined his head gravely. "Thank you," he said to his friend. "I appreciate the recommendation."

Bronwen decided Michael might well be right about the advisability of giving in. At least for the present. "Very well," she said coolly to Slade. "I'll accept your offer."

"Of marriage?" he asked with a grin that told her he knew perfectly well what she meant.

"No, of course not of marriage," she said irritably. "I was talking about your offer to move to your—your..."

"Place in the country," he finished for her. "It's not a private passion pit, if that's what you're thinking."

That thought had been at the back of her mind, but she wasn't going to let him know it. "Naturally not," she said, trying to sound haughty, and sounding a little wistful instead.

Michael chuckled. "It's the truth," he confirmed. "I've never known Slade to take a woman there."

"Perhaps," said Bronwen, who didn't like the turn of this conversation, "Slade would like to take *himself* there. Preferably at once."

"I might," he agreed. "Provided I receive some suitable appreciation."

"I am grateful." Bronwen struggled to assert good manners and proper gratitude over her habitual desire to deliver a smart kick to his seductive backside—or, failing that, to make love to him.

Watching her, Slade struggled with a habitual desire to kiss her—or, failing that, to take her by the shoulders and shake her.

"Then *show* me your appreciation," he ordered, spreading his arms out and pinning her with a challenging blue gaze. "Kiss me, Bronwen."

She ran her tongue helplessly over her lips. He looked so impossibly sexy and desirable, with his long body spread-eagled against the wall, that she knew that if Michael hadn't been there she would have done a great deal more than just kiss him.

As it was, she stood up slowly and walked toward him. He didn't move, and in the end, because it seemed less undignified than waiting for him to take the first step, she put her hands on his shoulders and kissed him as perfunctorily as she could.

At once he clamped his arms around her and swung her back against the wall. From that angle Michael couldn't see what his hands were doing—which was turning her light caress into a passionate exercise in foreplay that left her gasping and breathless, hungry for him, and very angry.

"Yes," he said when he had finished. "I think that will do for the present. You can thank me some more on Friday. I'll be around to pick you up about noon."

Bronwen was still struggling with her breath and her emotions, and she didn't answer.

Slade strolled into the bedroom, came back carrying a jacket, and sauntered across to the door.

"Take care of Michael," he said lightly. "And sweet dreams."

She closed her eyes, and when she opened them again he had gone.

"Horrible, self-centered, disgustingly arrogant man," she snapped, staring at the spot where he had been standing. "How can you bear having him for a friend, Michael?"

"You seemed pretty friendly with him yourself," her brother remarked mildly. "I'm surprised at you, little sister."

Bronwen twisted a button on her dress and turned around slowly. "He is attractive," she admitted. "I never realized just *how* attractive before. But he's still self-centered and impossible."

"So you're not marrying him?" said Michael, his dark eyes unusually thoughtful.

"Does it sound like it?"

"No. But I've never seen you so put out before."

"That's hardly an indication of approaching nuptials," she sniffed.

"You've sprouted a new crop of freckles," he replied inconsequentially.

"What's that got to do with anything?"

"I don't know. I thought it might have something to do with Slade."

"Really, Michael, Slade can cause more aggravation than any man I know, but even he can't manufacture freckles." She perched herself on the arm of the sofa and glared morosely over her brother's head at a sea gull on the railing.

Michael stared up at her with a small frown marring his boyish features. "What have you got against Slade?" he asked. "He's *not* self-centered, you know. He's done a lot for me over the years. And look how obliging he's being now—letting us have his apartment at great inconvenience to himself."

"It's a calculated obligingness," Bronwen asserted stubbornly. "He wants something."

"Yes. You. He said so."

"He doesn't want me."

"Believe me, my sweet little sister, Slade doesn't do anything he doesn't want to do. Least of all marry obstinate freckled redheads."

"He just likes getting his own way," insisted Bronwen. The button she had been twisting came away in her hand, and she shoved it into a pocket.

"Don't be daft. Why would he marry you, or anyone else, for a reason as trivial as that?"

"I don't know." Her gaze followed the sea gull's path as it lifted its wings and soared upward.

Michael's eyes narrowed. "You *are* in love with him, aren't you? I can tell."

"What would you know about it?" she demanded. "You've never been in love in your life."

To her surprise, he didn't laugh and shrug the accusation away.

"You could be right," he said slowly. "But I don't think so."

"Well, you ought to know."

"Yes, I ought. But it was years ago. There hasn't really been anyone serious since."

"So that hardly makes you an expert. At least not on love," said Bronwen with a touch of sarcasm.

"Perhaps not. But I still think you want to marry Slade."

"Maybe I do," she agreed grudgingly. "But I can't. He's not—not the marrying kind."

"He seems to think he is. And if he's made up his mind——"

"Michael Evans," said Bronwen, losing patience and jumping to her feet, "I am not going to marry Slade just because he's made up his mind. I've made mine up too, and he's not—not suitable."

"My goodness. She's holding out for Onassis," Michael gibed.

"He's dead," said Bronwen succinctly.

"So are you, officially."

"Not any more."

"Good," said Michael. "Because that means you can get me something to eat."

Bronwen looked at the clock. He was right, it was well past suppertime.

Mechanically she began to make the motions of preparing food, but her thoughts were occupied elsewhere. Michael, who knew Slade as well as anyone, insisted that his friend was not self-centered, and that if he said he wanted to marry her he meant it. Which might be true. But that didn't help much, she decided, cracking an egg briskly into a bowl. Because however much she loved him, she still couldn't marry a man who had deserted a young pregnant girl and left another man to raise his child. The older, more mature Slade she knew now might behave differently. But even so she would never be able to forget his cruel neglect of Jenny and his infant son. In the end those two would come between her and any true intimacy with Slade, because the seed of mistrust had been planted. It would always be there, growing, blighting her love for him.

Besides, she was by no means convinced that Slade felt any more for her than mild affection and a strong physical attraction.

"Stop mooning, finish cooking my dinner, and make up your mind to marry Slade," Michael broke into her gloomy musings. "If you keep breaking eggs into the sink, Bron, I'll have to go back to the hospital to eat." He brightened visibly. "There's an aide on the ward I rather fancy, but..."

Bronwen wasn't interested in his aide. She stared, aghast, at the river of bright yellow that was trickling glutinously down the drain. Damn. One thing she'd always prided herself on was her domestic skill. Surely Slade wasn't even affecting that?

But of course he was.

The next couple of days passed in a busy round of shopping, cooking, caring for Michael and trying to keep her mind off Friday, when Slade had promised to return. She wasn't sure if she was dreading it or looking forward to it. But she was quite sure that she found his absence hard to take. He didn't call, didn't contact them at all—and she missed him terribly.

She supposed he'd taken her at her word and canceled his plans for a wedding. Which, of course, was exactly what she wanted. Or so she tried to convince herself.

Friday came. It was raining, which didn't augur well.

Leaving Michael reclining on the sofa, Bronwen went out for a while to pick up groceries. When she returned, shortly after twelve, Slade was already there, lounging in a chair beside the invalid. He was wearing a dark suit and a crimson tie, but happily no pink carnation.

"You're late," he said.

"Late for what?" She took off her dripping raincoat and hung it in the cupboard beside the door.

"Don't tell me your memory is that short," he taunted. "We're getting married today, remember?" He gestured at a wheelchair, which was set up next to the sofa. "I've brought transportation for Michael."

"I'm best man, apparently," explained her brother.

Bronwen collapsed against the wall and ran a distraught hand through her damp red hair. "Slade," she said very slowly, "I don't know how I can make it any clearer, but I've told you at least half a dozen times that I won't marry you——"

"I know. It was getting to be such a bore that I decided to stay away for a few days." He stood up and moved swiftly toward her. "No," he continued pensively, putting his hands on her shoulders and running an appraising eye over her primly clad figure. "I'm afraid that housewifely print you're wearing won't do. The cream-and-gold, I think." He nodded. "Yes, definitely the cream-and-gold. Off you go."

She gaped at him, unable to believe he was serious, and before she knew what was happening he had spun her around, given her a brisk pat, and shoved her gently in the direction of the bedroom.

She stood with her back to him, fists clenched at her sides while she tried desperately to control her temper—which had only seemed to match her hair since Slade had reappeared in her life. In the end she decided there was nothing to be gained by holding it in check. A good old-fashioned tantrum might get his attention, and be the one thing that would dent his self-assurance.

Accordingly, she looked around for something to throw, and her gaze fell on a blue silk cushion. She picked it up, lifted it above her head, and at once Slade said, "I wouldn't. My aim is rather better than yours."

Which was true, she remembered. And she wasn't the foot-stamping type. On the other hand, reason didn't seem to work with Slade...

She threw the cushion back onto its chair. "All right," she said. "I've tried saying no, I've tried throwing things, I've tried saying I don't want to marry you. What do I have to do to convince you I mean it?"

"Oh, I'm quite convinced you mean it. Or think you do."

She shook her head helplessly. "Slade, I can't stop you kidnapping me, slinging me over your shoulder and forcing me to go with you to the altar. But I can, and I will, refuse to say "'I do'" when I get there." She looked straight into his ice blue eyes, which were entirely without expression. "If you don't want to embarrass a lot of people, I'd suggest that you take me at my word."

His reaction puzzled her. He didn't immediately try to assert his authority by quite literally slinging her across his shoulder, although he looked for a moment as though he'd like to. Nor did he ignore her words entirely and carry on as if she hadn't spoken. Instead he closed his eyes briefly, and when he opened them again she thought she saw pain, and a sort of anguished hopelessness. But the impression was gone very quickly, as his front of cool urbanity fell back in place.

"You're a stubborn little cat, aren't you?" he remarked, putting his hands in his pockets and rocking back on his heels.

"She always was, underneath that sweet and misleadingly pliable facade," said Michael from his place on the sofa.

"Mmm. So I've come to realize. Once she digs her claws in she needs a great deal of coercion to pull them out. Even when it's in her own best interests."

"Will you two stop talking about me as if I'm some kind of profoundly deaf feline?" Bronwen interrupted indignantly. "Slade, you'd better go and cancel that wedding."

She started to turn away, but found herself pinioned by his eyes. They were blue and hard, and they seemed to see right through her. "Bronwen," he said quietly, "I'm not in the habit of begging. If that's what you want I'm afraid you'll be disappointed. But that's not what you want, is it?"

She shook her head.

"Michael," said Slade over his shoulder, "don't raise your brotherly hackles, but your sister and I are going into the bedroom." He took Bronwen quite gently by the arm and moved her very firmly ahead of him. "I want to talk to her in private."

"Michael," cried Bronwen, "don't let him..."

"Nothing I can do about it," said Michael. "Don't worry, Bron, he won't eat you."

Bronwen wasn't worried about being eaten. She didn't think cannibalism was one of Slade's predilections.

"Now," said Slade, closing the door and leaning back against it with his arms crossed, "I want you to answer me something. Truthfully."

That wasn't at all what she'd expected. "What do you want to know?" she asked warily.

"Do you hate me."

"N-no. Of course not."

"But you don't love me?"

She dropped her eyes because she couldn't stand the perceptive intensity of his gaze. She couldn't produce an answer either. If she told him the truth the force of his personality could well end up propelling her to the altar.

"I see," said Slade slowly. "I think that answers my question."

She looked up, surprised, and saw that his lips were twisted in that familiar cynical smile.

"It's not that at all, is it?" he said, with devastating accuracy. "The reason you won't marry me is something that happened a very long time ago and for which you think I'm responsible."

She swallowed. "And aren't you?" she asked, hope springing up irrepressibly. If he denied it then perhaps she *could* marry him—even if he didn't truly love her. Her love would be enough for them both.

But he didn't deny it. Instead he lifted a hand, twisted a lock of her hair, and said sternly, "Can't you trust me, Bronwen? You've shared my home and my bed, you've known me for a great many years..."

Yes, she had known him. Known the reckless youth, her brother's friend—and her own lover. But if he was not responsible for Jenny's plight then surely he had only to say so? And he wouldn't.

"No," she said, shaking her head and staring at his crimson tie. "How can I trust you, Slade? You won't deny what happened."

She saw his chest rise beneath the severe dark cloth. "All right," he said, the harshness in his voice making her swallow. "Then what if we accept that I'm guilty as charged? It happened a long time ago. It's over. I want to marry you *now*, Bronwen."

"Why?" she asked, looking straight at him.

"Good heavens, woman, don't you know?" His grip on her hair tightened and he bunched it up behind her neck.

She moistened her lips, causing Slade to draw in his breath. "You're not going to tell me you love me?" she asked, opening her eyes very wide.

"No. I'm not, because you once told me you wouldn't believe me if I did."

That was true. She sighed, searching his face for something that wasn't there. Something that would answer the questions he wouldn't answer. But there was nothing, only a grim, set jaw, a flared, aquiline nose and blue eyes that glittered and gave nothing away.

"It's finished, Slade," she said, after a long, despairing silence. "I—I'm sorry. Thank you for—for everything." She gestured vaguely around the room. "Michael and I will move out, so you can have your apartment back——"

"You'll do no such thing. Michael's best interests lie in staying where he is and getting well. And he needs you to nurse him." Slade was all brisk business again now. There was no sign of the man who, just for a second, had seemed vulnerable and capable of being deeply hurt.

"Yes," said Bronwen miserably. "Michael does need me, of course. But I can't go on accepting your hospitality after——"

"You can and you will. Michael should be on his feet again in six to eight weeks' time. You can go home then—to your riotous existence running the shop in Pontglas."

"Don't," said Bronwen. "Don't sneer, Slade. I can't take any more."

His features didn't exactly soften, but he put his hand on the back of her head and pressed her face against his shoulder. After a while he put a finger under her chin and tilted it upward.

She stared at him wordlessly. His eyes were so incredibly blue, and they glittered with an unnatural brightness. He gave her a thin smile, and brushed his lips over hers. Briefly his arm tightened around her, then he said in a brisk voice, "You can pull your claws in now, little cat. I won't trouble you again, except to check on Michael now and then. He's in good hands."

He closed the door firmly behind him, as if he knew that she needed to be alone.

"For heaven's sake, Bron, stop mooning about in the bathroom and come and look at the sky. It's all pink and purple, and——"

"So are bruises, and I'm not mooning. I'm being sick."

"Oh." Michael listened to his sister choking and wondered if there was something he ought to do.

"What's the matter? I've heard of being lovesick, but——"

"I'm not lovesick." Bronwen swayed into the room, looking green. "I'm just sick."

"Oh," said Michael again. "That's the second time today. Have you got flu?"

"I don't know what I've got, but I wish I hadn't." She staggered to a chair and sank into it. "I was ill yesterday too."

"Hmm. I'll get you a cup of tea. Maybe you should see a doctor." He stood up and walked slowly into the kitchen.

Bronwen stared after him, thinking how much stronger he'd become in the last four weeks. He still avoided sudden or excessive movement, but when he had first come out of hospital he had barely been able to walk. Now he was fetching her cups of tea. *Her* health, on the other hand, seemed to have deteriorated markedly. For the past couple of days she had felt unusually tired, and her stomach kept behaving like a yo-yo. She smiled wanly. It was true that she missed Slade's presence terribly, and, in spite of the knowledge that she had made the right decision, she couldn't help regretting what she'd given up—regretting too that her nights were so lonely and bereft. But she certainly didn't believe *love* was making her sick. Sad, depressed, listless, yes. But not sick.

"Slade's coming over this evening," said Michael, handing her the freshly made tea. "Maybe he can recommend a doctor."

"I don't need a doctor."

"Yes, you do. That dried-pea complexion doesn't suit you."

"I suppose it doesn't." She took a sip of the tea, not caring much about her complexion. If Slade was coming over she ought to get ready to go out. But at the moment she didn't feel up to it.

He had visited them several times in the past weeks, to see Michael, and to ask if they needed anything. She was sure that he was also the source of the mysterious boxes of groceries that kept arriving, an opinion that was confirmed by Mrs. Bickersley, who kept a running tab on all deliveries.

On the days when Bronwen knew Slade was about to visit them she usually contrived to be out. But on two or three occasions now he had taken her by surprise, and there had been nothing she could do but endure his company.

She had expected that any meetings between them would be strained and awkward, but if they were the strain seemed to be entirely on her side. Slade made himself at home with easy affability and treated her with civility and casual charm—as if she were indeed no more to him than his friend's young sister.

Only once had she seen the mask slip, when she'd handed him a cup of coffee and their fingers touched. The spark that had sprung between them was instant and unmistakable. His eyes had seemed to darken, and she'd thought she saw a passionate regret in their blue depths that just for a second had looked as though it was tearing him apart. Then his features had smoothed out, and he'd smiled with cool politeness as he'd thanked her.

"I'd better go out," Bronwen said to Michael reluctantly as she sipped the tea he had brought her.

"You'd better stay in," he contradicted her. "You don't look well enough to walk."

She supposed he was right. She didn't *feel* well enough to walk.

By the time Slade strolled in at five o'clock, though, she was a great deal better.

"Bron's ill," Michael informed him the moment his friend came through the door. "She needs a doctor."

"I'm not. I don't," Bronwen protested quickly.

Slade ignored her and strode across the room to feel her head. "No temperature," he announced curtly.

"Of course not. I'm fine."

"She's not," said Michael. "She was a horrible shade of green this morning—and she's been sick."

"Hmm." Slade picked up the phone and dialed a number.

"What are you doing?" cried Bronwen.

He didn't answer, but a minute later she heard him talking in a clipped voice, and when he hung up the phone and turned around the appointment was already made.

"Dr. Swale will see you in an hour," he informed her.

"But I don't—I'm not—Slade, doctors don't see patients as late as this. Not unless they're really ill."

"Dr. Swale does. If I ask him to."

"Oh. But I don't *need* a doctor."

Slade looked at the clock. "I'll drive you there in about forty-five minutes," he announced, just as if she hadn't spoken. He turned to Michael. "How are you? More mobile these days, I see."

Bronwen lay back in her chair, mentally gnashing her teeth. Slade was taking over her life again, and she had a feeling that today she wouldn't have the strength to fight back.

She hadn't. When he glanced at his watch, scooped her out of the chair and carried her to the door as if she were no heavier than a cobweb she only managed a faint, "No, wait a minute..." before he was setting her down in the elevator. Then she was in the lobby, being carried past a bug-eyed Mrs. Bickersley to the Porsche.

"Thank goodness," said Slade. "She's safely at her command post and not out taking potshots at my car."

Bronwen smiled, and for the first time in weeks she actually felt like laughing. She might be green of face, and her stomach might resemble a yo-yo, but she was safe, contented, here with Slade's arms around her. He placed her gently in the passenger seat, and when he paused to tuck a blanket over her knees she had a sense that she had finally come home.

It wouldn't last, of course. How could it? And yet... Slade was being kind, he was caring for her—and he'd almost made her laugh. Could this really be the same callous hedonist who had deserted Jenny and his child?

She shook her head. For the time being it was all too much for her—and anyway they were already pulling up outside a white two-story building on West Broadway.

She struggled to get out, but Slade was there at once, opening the door, picking her up, and carrying her up a flight of white stairs.

Dr. Swale was a rotund little man with dark, puppy-dog eyes. After he had checked Bronwen over and pronounced that there appeared to be nothing seriously amiss he made a steeple of his fingers beneath his chins and asked briskly, "Is there any possibility you could be pregnant?" He threw a pointed glance toward the door behind which Slade could be heard strumming impatiently on the arm of a chair.

"Oh," said Bronwen. And then, as she felt the color wash from her face, "Oh-h, Doctor! No!"

CHAPTER EIGHT

"I SEE." Dr. Swale nodded. "I take it that means yes?"

"It was only once," whispered Bronwen.

"That's all it takes, I'm afraid."

Yes, she knew that. But...

"We'd better have some tests taken," said the doctor, who apparently believed in facing facts. "I'll write a referral to the clinic." He scribbled busily while Bronwen tried to collect her shattered thoughts.

Now that the doctor had actually put it in words, she was almost sure the tests would prove him right. It was early days yet, of course, but she knew some women did show symptoms early. And her breasts had felt unusually heavy of late...

"Well?" asked Slade as soon as they were back in the car. "What's the verdict?"

"I have to have some tests," she replied evasively.

"Right. I'll take you. When? Tomorrow?"

She nodded, and they drove home without further speech, although Bronwen was conscious that Slade's eyes kept slanting her way, as if he was tempted to ask a question but was holding back.

He left as soon as he'd seen her home, after promising to return the next day.

She spent a restless night, tossing back and forth, alternately too hot or too cold, while she listened to the rain pounding mercilessly on the roof. The sound found an echo in her head. It was pounding, too, as her mind went back and forth over the same track.

In other circumstances she would have been so happy to be bearing Slade's baby, she thought sadly. But as it was... She squeezed her eyes shut.

Perhaps, after all, it wasn't true. Perhaps she really did just have the flu.

But when she woke the next morning and felt her stomach roll over at the smell of Michael's coffee she knew there was no point in self-delusion. Besides, now that she thought about it... She began to count days on her fingers.

Yes, it was exactly as she'd feared.

Bronwen sat down at the breakfast table and fixed a bleary eye on the toast that a worried Michael had prepared for her.

"It won't bite," he assured her. "I know it looks a bit limp, but——"

"It's not that. I just don't feel very well."

It was true in more ways than one. She felt physically sick, of course, but her mental state wasn't much better.

What on earth was she going to do?

She was still wrestling with the problem when Slade arrived to take her for her tests, and she was no closer to a solution by the time he drove her home again and insisted on coming up with her to what was, after all, his own apartment.

"I'm all right now," she assured him. "I feel much better."

"Maybe so," said Slade, "but I still think you ought to go to bed."

"You have a one-track mind," she replied, without pausing to think.

Slade muttered something she couldn't hear. "Even *I* have my standards," he said bitingly. "Necrophilia isn't one of my vices, and at the moment you look about one step up from the grave."

"Thank you for those comforting words. In that case, my health must have improved considerably since I was first pronounced dead on arrival." Bronwen tried to bob a flippant curtsy, but she lost her balance and ended up in his arms. "Michael," she murmured, looking around anxiously for support.

"Serves you right for being smart," said Slade. "And Michael has gone for his checkup. Don't you remember?"

Oh. Yes, of course she did. He had left in a taxi, insisting that he was quite capable of managing the short journey on his own.

Slade's arms were still around her, but he didn't attempt to take advantage of her current weakness. "Come on," he said. "You ought to be lying down." He turned her toward the bedroom.

"No," cried Bronwen, resisting. "Slade, there's nothing wrong with me that—that..." She clapped a hand over her mouth. She had been going to say nothing that nine months wouldn't cure.

"You might as well say it," said Slade, changing direction and helping her onto the sofa.

She gulped. "Say what?"

"Weren't you about to say that there's nothing wrong with you that my absence from your life wouldn't make better?"

"No! I..."

Oh Lord, what was she to do? Did she want to marry him after all? And if she told him, would he still want to go through with it? He hadn't married Jenny when *she* was carrying his child.

Without her being aware of it, her expression hardened. It wasn't right that Slade should evade his responsibilities, not just once, but twice. Only... it wasn't right to marry without love either. She put her elbows on her knees and rested her forehead on her hands. Vaguely she was conscious that Slade had lowered himself down beside her.

"What is it, Bronwen?" he asked. His voice was low and compelling, the voice of a man who meant to have an answer.

She had to tell him. He had a right to know. And his child had a right to a father. Somehow she knew Slade would be a good father if he took on the responsibility—and her own feelings weren't important any more.

She lifted her head, not knowing that she wore the expression of a martyr stepping onto the scaffold. "I'm going to have a baby, Slade," she said in a clear, matter-of-fact voice. "The tests aren't back yet, of course, but there's not much doubt. You were right when you called me a stupid virgin. Now I'm going to pay for my stupidity."

Slade's face registered no emotion, but she saw a pulse throb just above the line of his jaw. "I see," he said after a long, agonizingly tense silence. "Am I right in assuming, then, that part of the payment will be marriage to the father of your child? In view of the fact that he's asked you, and is not in the habit of going back on his word?"

Bronwen swallowed and stared hopelessly at his ungiving features. He wasn't pleased. But he would still marry her.

"Yes," she said in a choked voice. "I will marry you, Slade. For the sake of the baby."

He nodded. "For the sake of the baby. Yes, naturally. I'll arrange it."

No emotion, no sign of the man who had held her and loved her for a short time one magical night. Just a brisk stranger making suitable arrangements.

Bronwen dropped her head back onto her hands and tried to stop her shoulders from shaking. As if in a dream, she thought she felt Slade touch her. But perhaps that was only an illusion... She had lost so many illusions these past few weeks.

"Don't worry." His cool voice came to her through a fog of misery. "We'll get married, but it needn't be in the full sense of that word. Though there was a time when I believed you and I..." He paused and she thought she heard him sigh, then decided that too must be illusion. When he spoke again his voice was colder than ever. "Never mind. You can rest assured I won't trouble you."

"Trouble...?"

She looked up, but he was already on his feet. "Take care of yourself, Bronwen," he said politely. "I'll let you know as soon as things are settled."

After he had gone she sat for a long time staring blankly down at the floor. Then she went into the bedroom to lie on the big bed and stare blankly up at the ceiling.

So, after all, she was going to marry Slade, mainly out of duty to her child. Which was strange in a way, because he too was marrying out of duty. It had shown in every set line of his face... No. She frowned. Perhaps it wasn't so strange after all. Slade was a man now, not the careless youth he had been eight years ago, and she, of all people, had reason to know that he could be considerate and kind, and unswervingly loyal to his friends. But he wasn't happy about marrying her. That was obvious from the way he had said their marriage didn't have to be a true one.

She pressed her knuckles into her eyes. Didn't he know that she wanted a full marriage? That the moments which had brought them to this pass had been the happiest moments of her life? She sighed heavily, and glared at the high white ceiling. If he did know it seemed he no longer cared.

The outside door opened, and Michael came in, whistling cheerfully. She got up to tell him the news.

Five days later Slade and Bronwen were married. Michael, now almost recovered, was best man. Bronwen, who knew no one she could ask to stand up with her, was grateful when Slade's unexpectedly plump and jolly secretary offered to be the other witness. They settled on a brief ceremony at a small chapel in Richmond set amid a garden of flowers. Or, rather, Slade settled on it, and Bronwen agreed with a listless lack of interest.

She hesitated briefly when the moment came to say "I do," but in the end she said it, very quietly. Slade glanced down at her and raised his eyebrows, but his own response rang out firm and clear.

Immediately after the service was over he helped his bride into the Porsche, thanked Michael and the kindly secretary, and drove away much too fast.

"Where are we going?" asked Bronwen, who hadn't cared enough to ask before.

"To my country place for a day or two. In the circumstances, I didn't think Greece would be appropriate." His voice was dry, uninterested. "Mrs. Doyle, my housekeeper, is back from her holiday, and she's been out there putting things in order. Incidentally, by the time we head into town again Michael tells me he'll have moved to his own apartment."

"Yes," said Bronwen, wishing he didn't sound so cool and uninvolved. "He told me that too."

"Did he also tell you he's going home to Wales? As soon as his assailant's trial is over?"

"Yes, but only to sell the shop for me," said Bronwen quickly. "He won't stay."

"Don't be too sure of that." Slade swung the car skillfully around a sharp bend and added with seeming irrelevance, "He didn't know Brice Barker was dead until I told him."

"Didn't he?" Bronwen wondered what Jenny's husband had to do with anything. "I suppose I must have forgotten to mention it to him."

"Mmm. I suppose you must."

She turned to look at him, but his enigmatic profile told her nothing, and he appeared to be concentrating on the road.

Two hours later, after a smooth ride, punctuated by polite references to the sunshine, the flat valley countryside and the possibility of rain, they pulled into a curving driveway at the end of which a large ranch-style house nestled in a clearing amid the trees. A bright green lawn stretched in front of it, and the house looked spacious, comfortable and expensive—as if its owner had gone to a great deal of trouble to make it fit into its surroundings.

"Do you like it?" asked Slade casually when his gaze fell on her startled face.

"Yes, it's lovely. I expected something—different."

"A huge Gothic mansion, I suppose, with chains, turrets, ghosts, secret passages and a garden of neglected roses in which I'm suspected of burying my indiscretions."

"Perhaps," said Bronwen wearily, hurt by his sarcasm, but too on edge to think of a cutting reply.

"Appropriate in its place, no doubt, but not my taste." Slade brought the car to a stop. "Besides, I prefer wildflowers to roses."

"And wild women," said Bronwen, immediately wishing she'd thought to swallow her tongue.

"Also appropriate in their place," agreed Slade dryly.

Bronwen forced herself not to kick a hole in his nearest shin, then wondered if perhaps she ought to. He would retaliate, of course, but anything would be better than the cool, distant composure with which he had treated her from the moment she had told him about the baby.

Mrs. Doyle opened the front door. She was a massive, pink-faced woman in a puce tracksuit that made her look like an amiable, but slow-moving beetroot.

She beamed at them, and Bronwen saw that her gums were as pink as the rest of her.

"Welcome to the happy couple," she intoned in a surprisingly deep voice. "It's about time somebody made an honest man of this young rascal."

Young rascal? Bronwen glanced quickly at Slade and made a successful effort not to choke.

He didn't blink an eye. "Bronwen doesn't think I'm honest at all," he told Mrs. Doyle impassively.

The housekeeper heaved her bulk around a half turn to fix a heavy-lidded gaze on Bronwen. "I don't believe it," she said after a moment. "No girl in her right mind would marry a young devil like you if she didn't trust you. You'll be enough of a handful as it is."

Bronwen felt herself reddening. "Slade's not convinced I am in my right mind, though," she explained, wondering if Mrs. Doyle was always this outspoken.

She was. "Hmm. Then he's a fool. Always suspected it. Never mind, he pays my wages." She gave Slade a comfortably pink smile. "Come on in now. I've left you a light supper in the breakfast room. Figured you'd want to be alone." She turned around and plodded down a short corridor, leaving Bronwen and Slade to follow in her considerable wake.

Bronwen took in the light, uncluttered breakfast room that overlooked a glade of foxgloves, and saw that, as Mrs. Doyle had promised, a cold supper awaited them on the table.

"I'll leave you two love birds to eat, then," she informed them. "You won't be wanting anything else." It was an announcement, not a question.

Slade gestured at the table after she'd gone. "We'd better do as we're told," he said lightly. "Mrs. Doyle doesn't take kindly to disobedience. I'll get our luggage in later."

Bronwen, still in her cream-and-gold finery, sat down doubtfully. "I didn't think you ever did what you were told," she said. "Umm—Mrs. Doyle seems nice, but not—er—not quite your style."

Slade smiled faintly. "She's exactly my style. A splendid cook, doesn't make a fuss about picking up after me, says what she thinks, and if she says she'll do something she does it. I wish I could say the same for all my employees." He passed her the salt and pepper. "The only mild fly in the ointment is her taste in tracksuits. They tend to be hard on the eyeballs."

Bronwen gave a small chuckle. She felt horribly tense and uneasy, as she had all day, but this amused, tolerant Slade she could cope with. It was the cool stranger who made her break out in unattractive goose bumps.

He continued to speak in the same light, superficial vein while they consumed Mrs. Doyle's excellent repast. As soon as they had finished their coffee he put down his cup and announced that he was off to collect their luggage from the car.

"I'll help," said Bronwen.

"You will not. My son and heir wouldn't like it."

"I'm not that fragile!" she exclaimed. "I haven't been sick at all today. And anyway he—she—may be a daughter." She stared uncomfortably at her empty plate, because it was the first time since she had told him about the baby that Slade had voluntarily brought the subject up.

"In that case, I hope she has your freckles," he replied surprisingly.

She looked up at once, but he was already walking out of the door.

When he came back empty-handed she knew the luggage had been safely stowed away. He jerked his head, indicating that she should follow him, and they set off down a wide corridor with floor-to-ceiling windows along one wall. Outside, an emerald expanse of lawn sloped down toward a small stream, which separated the garden proper from a wild tangle of uncultivated shrubs and grasses.

Slade came to a halt in a large, airy bedroom furnished in pine. Scatter rugs in his favorite green dotted the hard polished floor.

"Will this suit you?" he inquired. "Or would you rather see the other rooms first?"

Bronwen glanced at the comfortable double bed with the green patchwork quilt, and then at Slade. "You sound like the owner of a dubious hotel who has temporarily shifted the mice next door,'' she said glumly. "Yes, the room will suit me very well."

He nodded, ignoring her gibe. "Good. My room is just down the hall."

"Oh." She swallowed. "But——"

"For the sake of the baby, I believe you said." His features were carefully blank.

"Yes of course. Only——"

"Surely you don't want *more* than a father for your child?" he asked bitingly. "Especially one you don't particularly trust."

"I do trust you," she said slowly, staring at the hard line of his jaw.

Funny. It was true. She did trust him. What had happened in the past didn't seem to matter any more.

"Do you?" His lip curled in a way she didn't like. "But you still don't think much of my morals."

"I don't know." She looked desperately around the bright room, searching for help that wasn't there. Her gaze fell on an artist's conception of the stream at the bottom of the garden. It looked peaceful, and she let her eyes rest on the cool blue waters.

"You don't know," Slade repeated. "Well, I suppose that's progress." He sounded weary all of a sudden. "Sleep well, my dear." He touched a hand to her cheek.

She nodded. "I'll try," she said. Then added softly in Welsh, "*Nos da*, Slade."

His eyes seemed to gentle for a moment. "*Nos da*," he said quietly. "Good night, Bronwen."

It was only just after nine, much too early to go to bed. She sat down in a big easy chair by the window and watched a cluster of daisies sway gently back and forth in the breeze.

So this was how she was to spend her wedding night. Alone in this bright, inviting room. Why? She couldn't believe Slade didn't want her any more. Perhaps he didn't love her, but he was a virile, healthy man, and a short time ago he had wanted her very much. Now they were married. So why had he insisted on this idiotic farce of a honeymoon? Was it pride because she had once told him she couldn't trust him? Or was it that he imagined he was doing her a favor? Whatever it was, neither reason had anything to do with not wanting her. But he had been so cold lately...

She frowned and stood up quickly, feeling a sudden need for air.

The evening was warm and scented, and the grass beneath her bare feet was cool and soft. When she reached the stream she sat down, oblivious to the stains on her dress.

She sat for a long time, staring into the moving water, and when she heard a footstep behind her she jumped.

"You'll catch cold." Slade's voice was low and faintly censorious.

"Oh." She scrambled to her feet, feeling a little ridiculous. But then this whole situation was ridiculous, she realized suddenly. And *she* was allowing it to happen. "I was thinking," she told him, taking the arm he proffered and starting to walk back with him to the house.

"What about?" He didn't sound cold any more, only tired.

Bronwen took a deep breath. "About us," she said. "About this being our wedding night. Slade, I don't feel sick any more, and I don't want to spend it alone."

"No," he said. "I didn't think you did. Frankly, neither do I."

She stopped walking. "Then why...?"

"Because you're not ready to accept me as I am. I don't think you even know who or what I am. When—if—you do then..." He shrugged. "Then we'll see."

She wanted to say, "I do accept you. I do know who and what you are, and I love you in spite of it." But she couldn't get the words out, because Slade was walking on ahead and was once again the cool and passionless stranger. Not a husband who was anxious to claim his bride.

When they reached the house she seized his hand again, hoping her touch would convey the message she hadn't spoken. But he shook her off, and she knew that if she didn't stop him he would go into his room and shut the door in her face.

"Slade," she managed to choke out. "I do accept you. What you did—it doesn't matter..."

His eyebrows lifted. "What I did?"

"I mean not marrying Jenny——"

"Not marrying the mother of my child doesn't matter? You surprise me, Bronwen."

She hated the bitter cynicism in his voice, hated the way he looked at her, all cold and supercilious and sneering. She would have hated everything about him in that moment if only she hadn't loved him so much.

"I mean," she continued valiantly, "that I can accept now that what happened in the past is over. You said that yourself. We're married now, and I'm going to have your baby. Can't we—can't we start afresh, Slade, make something good grow out of all this hurt?"

"You mean, I suppose," said Slade icily, "that you forgive me."

Why did he sound so angry? As though *she* were the one in need of absolution?

"Yes, I do," she replied, knowing it was the wrong thing to say. "And now I'm wondering if perhaps you can't forgive *me* for—well, for forgiving you."

He gave a short, contemptuous laugh that wasn't really a laugh at all. "Amateur psychology," he said dismissively. "Don't try to analyze me, Bronwen."

"I don't want to," she said, gazing up at him with something like despair. "I only want to love you. I know—I know you're not the same man you were eight years ago."

"I'm exactly the same man," he snapped. "A little older and a lot wiser—but nothing about me that matters has changed at all."

Bronwen shook her head, not even pretending to understand, and once again Slade turned abruptly away.

She grabbed his arm, tugging at it, forcing him to look at her—and when he did, and she saw his eyes, she almost wished she'd let him go. They were empty, opaque, so totally without expression that he hardly seemed human any more. And she felt as if there were a band around her throat, choking the life from her as well.

Desperately she lifted a hand to his frozen cheek.

He closed his eyes, and a ripple of emotion moved beneath the flat mask of his face.

Very slowly Bronwen coiled her arms around his neck.

For what seemed an aeon he just stood there, letting her fingers caress the taut muscles of his neck, letting them stroke gently along his jaw and across his lips...

Then with a deep groan he bent his head and pulled her to him, kissing her with a hungry urgency that made her cry out as her body responded joyfully to his.

The kiss deepened, he murmured, "Bronwen," and began to lead her backward toward his room. But when he reached behind him for the handle, and didn't find it, he raised his head again and paused to look into her eyes.

Even as she watched him, the hunger and the longing faded, and his features seemed to close up.

"No," he said harshly, holding her away. "I'm sorry, Bronwen. I shouldn't have let you touch me."

"Let me—— Slade, what are you talking about? Have you—have you forgotten I'm your wife?"

"I haven't forgotten." He spoke with such grim despair that, hearing him, Bronwen knew she had lost.

For a moment she refused to accept what her heart was telling her. She stared at him, hoping against hope that she was wrong. But she wasn't wrong. There was a rigidity about him, a cold withdrawal that she didn't know how to overcome.

She started to say, "Slade . . ." then stopped as the futility of it overwhelmed her. She would have given up then if Mrs. Doyle, swathed in a vast pink dressing gown, hadn't ambled into the hallway, stopped dead, and muttered disgustedly, "Huh. Things are coming to something when newlyweds can't even get as far as the bedroom without squabbling." She puttered past them and disappeared into her room, still muttering.

Slade stared after her and brushed an arm across his forehead. "She's right," he said. "I don't want to squabble with you, Bronwen."

"Neither do I."

He nodded. "I know. So please, just go to your room." His lips twisted painfully. "And sleep well."

Her shoulders sagged, and she turned her back on him, unable to bear any more. "Yes. I'm going to bed now,'' she said quietly, and walked with dragging steps down the hall to her solitary bedroom.

In the old days, she thought despairingly, he would have asked her if she wanted company. But she knew he wouldn't tonight.

He didn't, and her wedding night was long, lonely and desolate. She wondered if his was too, but, remembering his bleak dismissal of the love she'd offered, she supposed he must be sleeping soundly.

She bit her lip, swallowed hard, and refused to allow the tears to flow.

The next few days were equally long, filled with Slade's presence, but still unbearably lonely. He was there most of the time, seeing that she ate regularly and well, and that she had books and music to keep her busy. When she wanted to swim in the big pool, or walk in the countryside, he accompanied her, and revealed a surprising knowledge of botany and absolutely nothing of himself. But he was courteous and considerate in a way he had never troubled to be during the early days in his apartment, and she missed the old, bantering Slade who had made her laugh as often as he'd made her want to hit him.

''What's the matter with you young people? I've never seen anything like it.'' Mrs. Doyle, in an olive green tracksuit trimmed with scarlet poppies, accosted Bronwen in the breakfast room one morning after Slade had gone upstairs to take a shower.

''Like what, Mrs. Doyle?'' Bronwen still found the housekeeper's outspokenness at bit startling, but she was beginning to appreciate her worth.

''Honeymoon,'' said Mrs. Doyle succinctly. ''Separate rooms. Ridiculous.''

As Bronwen wholeheartedly agreed with her, she didn't see much point in arguing.

"I know," she said. "I think so too."

The housekeeper shook her head. "Then don't put up with it. Your husband's crazy in love with you. It's as plain as that straight nose on his face."

"Oh, no," said Bronwen quickly. "I don't think he is. He—he says I don't even know him."

"Hmm. And do you?"

"Well, I..." Bronwen stared at the bulky figure standing over her. Maybe, just maybe, from this unlikely source... She put a hand over her eyes and thought for a very long time.

"Yes," she said at last, experiencing, not a blinding light exactly, but something akin to the thump that had shot through her as a child, when Michael, with deliberate devilment, had abandoned his end of the seesaw. "Yes, Mrs. Doyle, I think I do. Excuse me. I—I have to do something."

"I should hope so," sniffed Mrs. Doyle, turning her poppy-covered back. "About time."

What Bronwen had to do was not what the housekeeper probably had in mind. First she had to think. Very seriously. She hurried into her chastely single room and plumped herself down in the chair.

Gradually, as she gazed through the window at the daisies, her thoughts fell into place like notes of music—and the knowledge that had been growing in her for weeks without her realizing it at last gave her the answer she needed.

Slade might be arrogant and a little ruthless, too used to getting his own way—but he was not irresponsible and self-centered. On the contrary, he was honorable and strong-minded. Tough both in mind and in body. In short, he was a man who would have been incapable of deserting the mother of his child. The rumors had been just that. Rumors. It wasn't possible that Slade could be the father of little Bobby.

She stared blindly at the yellow daisies, her eyes misted with tears. No wonder he had been so distant. No wonder he had been reluctant to make love to a woman who thought him guilty of an act which he found thoroughly repugnant. And no wonder he had married her anyway, in spite of her lack of belief in him. She should have understood what kind of man he was when he had told her about Valerie's having a husband, and how he preferred his women unattached. Perhaps that *was* when she had begun to know...

She twisted the sash of her new silk robe, knowing there was still one huge question unanswered. If Slade wasn't Bobby's father, why had he refused to say so outright? What possible reason could he have had for remaining silent?

After a while, as the daisies bobbed busily in the breeze, she knew there could be only one answer. Loyalty. Loyalty to someone he cared about, someone he wouldn't want to hurt...

She knew now who had fathered Jenny's baby. Perhaps, subconsciously, she had known for a very long time—which was why she had been so ready to accuse Slade.

She closed her eyes and let out a low cry of pain.

CHAPTER NINE

BRONWEN went to look for Slade, but she couldn't find him.

"He drove off in that racing car of his," said Mrs. Doyle, who had changed into a neon yellow tracksuit. "Said he had some business to attend to, but he looked to me more as if he was looking for someone to kick." As usual, the housekeeper wasn't bothering to mince her words.

"Oh," said Bronwen. "Did he say when he'd be back?"

"Lunchtime. Maybe. Strikes me we'll all be better off if he stays away."

Bronwen didn't think so. She needed desperately to talk to him, whatever foul mood he happened to be in. But there wasn't much she could do about it. Except, perhaps, phone Michael.

She picked up the phone in the long sunroom that overlooked the garden.

"Hello." Michael's voice was clear, healthy and cheerful.

"It's me," said Bronwen.

"Hi. You sound as if you're being . strangled. Where's Slade?"

"Not strangling me. According to Mrs. Doyle, he's out looking for someone to kick."

"Hmm?" Michael sounded puzzled. "What's wrong, Bron?"

She twisted the cord of the telephone. "Michael..."

"Yes? Spit it out."

Bronwen moistened her lips, which had gone un-usually dry. "Michael, are you—are you Bobby Barker's father?" There. She knew she was croaking like a frog with laryngitis, but at least she had managed to get the words out.

Michael answered with less reluctance than she'd expected. "Yes. Yes, I am, Bron. I thought perhaps you knew. Did Jenny tell you?"

She slumped against the wall. "No, nobody told me. I figured it out for myself. I—I always thought Slade was the baby's father. Everyone did."

She heard Michael expel a startled breath.

"*Slade!*" he exclaimed. "Why Slade? Hell, Bron, the man practically scalped me when he knew. I hate to admit it, but Slade wouldn't have got Jenny in that predicament. Unless he was very sure he could marry her."

"I know. I should have realized."

There was a pause during which both of them col-lected their thoughts, then Michael's voice came to her with a certain diffidence. "Bron, is that what's been the trouble between you and Slade? I didn't know. I know I left Pontglas in a hell of a hurry, without telling anyone why, but that was because I didn't want to hurt Mother. I hoped she wouldn't find out, only I never imagined anyone would think... That is, I didn't mean..."

"No," said Bronwen tonelessly. "You never do."

"But how could I help it?" he objected. "You didn't tell me."

"You could have had the decency to stay away from Jenny when you knew she was engaged to another man," said Bronwen sharply. Dear Lord, her brother had always been irresponsible, but this was altogether too much.

"But she wasn't," protested Michael. "At least, she didn't want to be. Jenny and I always cared for each other, but her parents didn't approve of me, and . . ."

"I don't blame them." Bronwen was fast losing patience.

"No, but you don't understand. I know I wasn't very sober and settled, but I loved Jenny. I would have made her happy. Her parents only wanted her to marry Brice because he was older and richer and his father was running for mayor."

That much was true, thought Bronwen. She remembered how the Prices had bragged about their daughter's engagement.

"All the same, they couldn't force Jenny to marry him," she pointed out.

"No, but they wore her down in the end. Made her believe she couldn't be happy with me. Jenny wasn't strong willed in those days. I don't know how she is now, but at that time she was sweet, and easily influenced. And only seventeen, after all."

"Is that how you managed to get her pregnant?" Bronwen was beginning to sympathize with Mrs. Doyle's habit of going straight for the jugular.

"Bron! No, it wasn't. I tell you we loved each other. If you want the truth, I still do. Now that I know Brice is dead, I'm going home to see if—if she still wants me."

"Oh." Bronwen digested that. "But Michael, if you felt so strongly, why in the world did you run away in the first place? And why did Slade let you?"

"He didn't. I phoned him from London, and after telling me what a fool I was, and that I deserved to have my butt kicked severely, he finally realized I wasn't going to come home. That's when he agreed to help me. Said something about my being a babe

in the woods, and that if I was set on being an idiot
he'd do his best to see I did a proper job.''

"Of being an idiot?"

"I suppose so. Mum and Dad never approved of
him, but really he was the one who kept me out of
trouble—most of the time."

Yes, thought Bronwen. Except the one time it mattered. The time when Michael was busy putting Jenny
in the family way. She smiled wryly into the phone.
Even Slade couldn't have been expected to prevent
that.

"I can see why Slade felt obliged to go on keeping
you out of trouble," she said pensively. "He's that
sort of person. But I don't really see why you had to
run away—and make Mother and Dad so unhappy.
Why didn't you stay and fight for Jenny?"

"I tried. We didn't know she was pregnant until
after she gave in to the pressure and agreed to get
engaged to Brice."

"But surely that would have been a reason to break
off the engagement?"

"He wouldn't let her. Fellow was in love with her.
Said he'd bring up the child himself, and if I didn't
get out of town fast he'd break every bone in my body.
Which he would have been quite capable of doing.
He also told Jenny that, if she didn't encourage me
to leave, he'd start on *her* bones. That's what finally
decided me. She was scared, not even sure she loved
me any more, and she begged me to go away, not to
keep in touch. That's why I didn't know..." He
stopped, cleared his throat noisily, and went on.
"Anyway, I figured that with me out of the picture
she had a decent chance of being happy. I don't think
Brice was a naturally violent man. He was just in love.
But he wasn't one to give up."

Which Michael had been. But he was older now, she thought, maybe stronger. Perhaps, with Jenny's love, and with a child to look after, he might finally learn to be a man.

Bronwen sighed. "Well, good luck to you both," she said, meaning it.

Yes, Michael would need luck, she mused as she put down the phone. But *she* would need it even more. Slade had a lot to forgive, and he'd never struck her as a man who forgave others their trespasses with a good grace.

He came back at lunchtime, looking a bit like Jupiter stepping down from his throne to cause trouble for the first unlucky mortal who crossed his path.

"Huh," said Mrs. Doyle, who was standing beside Bronwen at the kitchen window. "That one didn't find the person he wanted to kick."

"I think it's me, actually," said Bronwen in a small voice.

"Hmm. Very likely. But he'll have me to answer to if he tries it." Mrs. Doyle picked up a marbled rolling pin and waved it threateningly at the ceiling. Then she put it down again and added almost regretfully, "He won't try it, though. He's not the type."

Bronwen, who a moment before had been ready to burst into tears, discovered she was laughing instead.

"You're a tonic, Mrs. Doyle," she chuckled, wiping a hand across her eyes. "Thank you."

As she went to find Slade, who had disappeared around the side of the house as if he were pursued by bats from hell, she heard Mrs. Doyle mutter caustically from behind her, "Tonic indeed. Castor oil, I guess you mean."

Bronwen found Slade leaning against an oak tree down by the stream. He was wearing cream colored denims and a yellow shirt. His hands were deep in his pockets, and he was staring out over the wild landscape with a look of utter desolation in his eyes. Watching him, she felt like bursting into tears.

"Slade," she said quietly, moving up beside him. "Slade, I'm sorry."

He turned his head, but the bleak expression remained. "Why are you sorry?" he asked with an indifference that made her blanch.

"Because I didn't trust you. About Jenny."

He turned away again. "I see. You've been talking to Michael."

She nodded. "Yes. But I didn't need to."

"Didn't you? Are you trying to tell me you suddenly saw the light? That a voice from on high, presumably Michael's, declared my innocence to you out of a cloud?"

He spoke with such bitterness that Bronwen gasped. "No," she said as gently as possible. "I did some thinking, that's all. Finally. And I used my head, instead of letting myself be blinded by family loyalty."

"The only thing likely to blind you around here is Mrs. Doyle's yellow tracksuit," he said grimly.

Bronwen narrowed her eyes. Was he trying to cover his feelings with a facade of flippancy? Or was he teasing her? No, surely not. Not now, of all times, when she was trying to make amends for her mistakes. But it would be just like him.

She studied him more closely, and decided he definitely wasn't teasing. The deep grooves beside his mouth weren't carved from laughter.

"Slade, I'm trying to tell you I'm sorry."

"Fine. You've told me."

"*Slade . . .*"

"Look," he said, moving away from the tree and turning to face her. "You've apologized. I've accepted your apology. Now let's leave it."

"But you haven't accepted anything. You're angry, and I don't blame you. Of *course* I should have understood that you were the last person on earth who would be likely to take advantage of Jenny. But Slade, Michael's my brother. It never occurred to me——"

"Until he told you."

"*No.* I did talk to Michael, but I didn't *need* to. I looked for you first, but I couldn't find you." She twisted a lock of red hair around her finger. "The fact is, the truth must have been dawning on me for a long time. It just wasn't until today that everything seemed to fall into place. I—I love you, Slade. I think—I hope—is there any chance you might happen to love me too?" She stretched out a hand, her eyes deep gray and enormous. But he stepped back as if her touch would strike him dead.

"Of course I love you," he replied, so harshly that Bronwen jumped. "Why do you think I wanted to box your ears that day I thought you'd fallen into the canyon? Why do you think I asked you to marry me, for heaven's sake? Would you believe that after you refused me I half hoped you *would* get pregnant, just so you'd have to change your mind? Oh, I knew you didn't have a high opinion of my character, but I thought, if I could persuade you to marry me, sooner or later you would have to understand that I'm not a man who loves lightly—or strews the landscape with unwanted brats." He gazed bleakly at the tops of the trees, and the bitterness of his tone made her wince. "I couldn't destroy your faith in your brother, Bronwen. What would you have thought of me if I'd cravenly defended myself by shifting the blame onto Michael?''

"It's where it belonged," she said quietly. She was shattered by Slade's unexpected harshness. It defeated her, although she understood now that her accusations must have hurt him intolerably...

Her rambling thoughts came into focus suddenly, almost as if she had indeed heard a voice coming out of a cloud.

Slade had just said he loved her. Surely that was the only thing that mattered?

"You said you loved me," she whispered. "Please, can't we start again?"

"I thought so at one time," he replied, so coldly that she wanted to scream. "As I told you, I was convinced that if you married me you would learn to love more than the part of me you happen to be able to see." His mouth twisted cruelly. "I knew you had no problems with that."

"But I do love——"

"Yes, so you said. I suppose Michael's revelations *would* put a different light on the matter."

"Slade, I loved you almost from the beginning. And Michael only told me what I already knew." She resisted the urge to plead when she saw the unforgiving line that was his mouth.

He didn't answer, and when his lips curled in a faint sneer she felt helpless. His hands were still in his pockets, and his head was thrown back to expose the corded sinews of his throat. A soft breeze was lifting his hair, blowing it seductively across his forehead.

Bronwen stared hopelessly, longing to touch him, to run her hands through that hair, and down his back, over his superb hips and thighs. But there was nothing remotely encouraging about his stance, and she knew that if she reached for him he would reject her. And suddenly she couldn't bear his rejection any longer.

With a moan like that of an animal in pain she stumbled away across the grass.

Her eyes were blurred with tears, she couldn't see where she was going, and after a while she became aware that the ground beneath her feet was no longer grass, but hard pavement. In her misery she had staggered out onto the road. The stream, wending its way from the garden, was tumbling and whispering beside her.

She paused, dashed a hand across her eyes, and in that split second saw something blue-and-gray loom up out of the mist that was her vision.

A bus. The roaring thing rushing toward her with a squeal of brakes was a *bus*.

She waved her arms frantically, stepped backward, felt a blast of air on her face and heard the howl of an engine—then her feet skidded from beneath her on a patch of mud and she was falling toward the sound of murmuring water.

It wasn't a long fall, and the stream was cool, refreshing. There were weird colored lights in front of her eyes. She watched them curiously, not caring that her blue skirt and bright print blouse were saturated. Not caring about anything much any more...

"Bronwen. Bronwen, darling, wake up."

She was soaked to the skin, but she wasn't in the stream any more. Slade's voice seemed surprisingly close. Reluctantly she lifted an eyelid. No wonder he had sounded close. She was in his arms, and he was carrying her up the steps to the house. His yellow shirt was as wet as her blouse, and the look in his eyes was no longer cold and derisive, but warm and fierce with concern. Had she died after all and gone to heaven?

Deciding that in any case she was where she wanted to be, she shut her eyes again with a contented murmur...

"Bronwen, I said wake up."

"Mmm?"

She was in her own bed now and, although she felt warm under the covers, she didn't seem to have any clothes on. Slade's voice, commanding and insistent, was shouting into her ear.

"You make too much noise," she mumbled.

"I'll make more than noise if you don't open up those eyes. You've got to stay awake, Bronwen. You hit your head."

"I know. It was nice."

She heard a groan of exasperation. "If I have to force you to stay awake you won't find it nice at all," he threatened.

"Won't I?" she murmured. She felt his hand curling around her hip, and added, "I like that."

"Well, you won't if you keep this up. I said, open your eyes."

He sounded so fierce that she decided it might be more peaceful to do as he said.

"That's better." The scowl between his brows cleared at once. He shook his head. "Have you any idea what a great trial you are to me, Bronwen Slade?"

"Bronwen Slade? My name's... Oh. No, it's not, is it?"

He smiled, and it was a smile of such tender amusement that her heart seemed to melt like toffee. "No, my love. It isn't."

She smiled back dreamily. "You called me your love. And your darling."

"Because you are. So please don't try to kill yourself again."

"I didn't . . ." Her smile faded into a frown, which hurt her head. "You're being human."

"I thought I *was* human. Dr. Swale seemed convinced of it on my last visit."

"No, I mean, you were so aloof down there by the stream . . ."

He smoothed her hair gently off her face. "I know." Heavy eyelids dropped down to shield his eyes. "I'm afraid, my dear, that after several days of marriage to you, which I spent wanting to murder you slowly because I couldn't bring myself to make love to you, I wasn't in any mood to be mollified by an apology that I felt you shouldn't have needed to make in the first place." He smiled ruefully. "You see, I've loved you for a very long time, even if eight years ago I was too restless and too footloose to acknowledge it to myself. Then I met you again, and I knew at once what I wanted. And, very foolishly, I thought that if I married you everything would have to work out. But it didn't. *I* didn't, because I found I couldn't make love to a woman who despised me—however much I wanted her, and however much she lusted after my body." He leered self-mockingly. "In other words, I found myself in a quandary."

She nodded, and then wished she hadn't. It made her head hurt. "I do see that. But—what made you decide to be mollified after all?"

"I dare say I'd have come around to it in any case. But the process was speeded up when I followed you out to the road and watched you trying to kill yourself before my eyes." He kissed the tip of her nose. "I thought the beginning was about to become the end. That everything had come full circle, and you were really going to be killed by a bus, as it said in the paper. And it would have been my fault. I knew right then that I didn't want to live in a world where there was no carrot-haired woman around to drive me crazy."

"Oh, Slade," she murmured, putting out her hand and touching it to his still wet shoulder. "I am so sorry."

He picked up the hand and kissed the back of it. "It was as much my doing as yours. I realize that now. Of course you believed in your brother. And you had no reason not to believe all those rumors, especially when I refused to deny them. I should have found a way of convincing you without damaging Michael's reputation. The fact is, I was too damn proud to try."

She pulled her fingers from his and ran them over the wet fabric stretched across his chest. An urgent need stirred in her stomach. "I hurt you," she said softly. "And there's nothing wrong with pride. If Michael had had more of it maybe all of us would still be in Pontglas." She made a face. "On the other hand, it's probably because you were so—so noticeable, and seemed so much more invincible than Michael, that everyone thought you were the guilty party."

"Maybe." He lowered his head, and then raised it again quickly. "Was it a great shock to you? About Michael?"

She sighed. "No, I don't think so. Not really. A great disappointment, of course. But he's my brother and I have to stand by him."

"Mmm. I know. I'm his friend and I feel the same way." He frowned, and returned to a point she'd made earlier. "I doubt if I would have stayed in Pontglas, though, Michael or no Michael. I was getting restless by then anyway. Ready to move on. Searching for something, I suppose.''

"What were you searching for?''

He shrugged. "Love. The one thing I'd always had to fight for. First from my parents, who loved the bottle better, then from Aunt Nerys, who had her own brood to attend to. And finally, my beloved redhead, from you—who proved the greatest challenge of them all.''

"You won,'' she said softly. "You defeated me, Slade.''

"No,'' he said, bending down to kiss her lips. "I'd never want to defeat you, beautiful Bronwen. I think both of us enjoy the battle too much.''

Bronwen laughed. "I never thought of myself as an Amazon,'' she said wryly.

He shook his head. "Not an Amazon, my love. More like a killer mosquito. Once you get under a man's skin you're an endless itch.''

"Thanks. You make me sound like the measles.''

He grinned. "Not measles. Just a persistent itch. One that I intend to deal with the moment you tell me you're up to it.''

"I'm up to it.'' She put her arms around his neck.

Slade laughed, and swung himself down beside her, cradling her head on his shoulder. "Remember the Chinese garden?'' he asked, surprising her by his swift change of mood.

"Of course. Why?''

"Because I believe I've found another place of pleasure for the heart.''

"Where?'' She ran her finger across his cheekbone.

"Here. Anywhere I am with you.''

Bronwen smiled. "My heart tells me the same. Did you know you're all wet?'' she added irrelevantly.

"Mmm. I am, aren't I? And you're all naked. Which is as it should be."

Mrs. Doyle, passing the door a few minutes later, and hearing a man's low murmur, followed by a woman's breathless laugh, gave a satisfied nod and muttered out loud that it was about time the honeymoon got itself off the ground.

If either occupant of the bedroom had heard her they could have assured Mrs. Doyle that the honeymoon was not only off the ground, but it was also soaring to celestial heights.

"Mrs. Bickersley has a problem," Bronwen whispered to Slade.

He raised his champagne glass and smiled wryly. "Mrs. Bickersley *is* a problem, my dear. And she's all yours."

Bronwen chuckled, and glanced around the bright sunroom, which today was filled with a chattering throng of well-wishers. Over by the window, Mrs. Bickersley was glaring at a sheet of writing paper and waving it at anyone misguided enough to come near her.

Six weeks had passed now since that day when Bronwen had fallen into the stream and Slade had discovered that life without his carrot-haired bride would be unthinkable. Today they were holding the reception that he had promised her on the night he had first proposed. Tomorrow they were leaving for Greece.

Most of the guests were Slade's friends, of course, which was why Bronwen had laughingly insisted that Mrs. Bickersley had to be included.

"She's a familiar face," she explained. "Apart from your secretary and Mrs. Doyle, I've hardly had a chance to meet your friends."

"You will. And you'll make your own. Right now I want you to myself."

And he'd had her to himself, more or less, except when business and Michael had intervened.

To Bronwen's regret, Michael had left Vancouver the week before. The moment the court case was over, and his attacker convicted, he had caught the first available plane to London. Just two days ago they had received a phone call telling them that he had married his Jenny, and that little Bobby was the most wonderful son any father could possibly wish for. When he'd added that he planned to take over the family shop Bronwen had found herself wiping away a tear.

She was certain that, wherever her parents were in the cosmos, somehow they knew, and were happy.

"What *is* in that piece of paper Mrs. Bickersley is waving about?" Slade asked idly, bringing Bronwen back to the present with a start.

She giggled and buried her nose in her glass.

"Champagne is supposed to be sipped, not sniffed," he said dryly. "What's so amusing?"

Bronwen composed herself. "Apparently she's received a very fancy letter from a senior citizens' home she visited in the process of being a dedicated people person. They have just informed her that her explanation that she only drove into their fence because another car was parked too closely behind her isn't good enough. She's mortally offended because they wrote that, according to legal advice, if their road is blocked for one reason or another she cannot simply forge ahead and make her own road."

"And of course she doesn't see why not, as it's exactly what she's always done." Slade put his glass down hastily, and turned his back as Mrs. Bickersley waved from across the room. "My sympathies to the senior citizens," he murmured over his shoulder—which, she noticed, was shaking suspiciously.

Mrs. Doyle stalked up to them, resplendent in an emerald-and-orange culotte dress with a deep V at the front, which had already given Bronwen some nervous moments.

"The caterers are mixing caviar with avocado," she announced in a voice redolent with dudgeon. "And they've put smoked salmon pâté beside the olives. Mrs. Slade, their color combinations are atrocious. Atrocious," she repeated emphatically. "I should have done the catering myself."

Slade, with a hand to his mouth, beat a hasty retreat from the room.

By the time Bronwen had a chance to talk to him again everyone had left but the housekeeper, who was still grumbling noisily in the kitchen.

"Alone at last," said Slade, coming up behind her as she gazed dreamily out of the window.

"Except for Mrs. Doyle."

"True. And little Slade." He put his hand over her stomach.

"What if he's little Bronwen?"

"No, I have a feeling this one is going to be a boy. The five after that will be Bronwens."

"*Five*!" she exclaimed. "Slade, if you're thinking of founding a dynasty I promise you they'll all be boys. And I'm going to call each one of them Emlyn."

"You *are* asking for trouble, aren't you?" he said, with a retaliatory glint in his eye.

Bronwen smiled mischievously. "Maybe. It depends what kind of trouble."

"Hmm." He wrapped both arms round her waist, which was thickening slightly, and rocked her back against his chest. "Mrs. Doyle is busy in the kitchen, finding fault," he said pensively. "She'll be happily occupied for hours."

"Yes, I suppose so." She turned in the circle of his arms and ran her fingers through the sunlight gilding his hair. "Slade . . . ?"

"Mmm?"

"Isn't it lucky that newspapers make mistakes? If they didn't I wouldn't be here."

He closed his eyes. "Yes. It's also lucky that that bus didn't hit you. Please don't tempt fate a third time, Bronwen Slade, or I'll have to keep you locked in the bedroom."

"Well, as long as you're there too, I could live with that." Bronwen batted her eyelashes at him, and started to unbuckle his belt. She smiled reminiscently. "Do you remember coming down that hospital corridor and accusing me of being alive?"

"Vividly. I also remember you thanking me for confirming the fact. It left me remarkably confused."

"Did it?" She ran her hand slowly up the inside of his thigh.

"You," said Slade, "are about to get that trouble you've been asking for. And yes, it did. I couldn't make up my mind if I wanted to laugh or to shake you."

"You didn't do either."

"I know." He grinned wickedly, and before she had time to gasp he had swept her up into his arms. "I did something much more sensible instead."

"Yes," said Bronwen as he carried her along the passageway. "You married me. Was that sensible?"

"I shouldn't think so," he replied honestly, kicking open the door of the bedroom. "But something tells me sensible isn't likely to have a lot to do with my life from now on."

"You may be right," she agreed, glancing over his shoulder. "On the other hand, *I* still have a healthy sense of self-preservation, and I don't think it's a good idea to throw caution completely to the wind."

"Why not?" His eyes met hers, bold, confident and possessive.

"Well, I'm not sure this is the right time and place——"

"Any time is the right time and place——" He stopped as his stunned gaze fell on a scarlet bedspread with silver-and-gold tassels. Behind it was an open cupboard filled with tracksuits. Very colorful tracksuits.

"Oh, no," he said. "*No*. I always knew you could drive me crazy, my love, but——"

"But you didn't think I could make you forget yourself to the point of invading Mrs. Doyle's boudoir? Otherwise known as tracksuit heaven?"

Slade shook his head. "With you all things are possible," he replied, reversing smartly back the way he had come. "Which is what I'm about to prove to you right now."

He kicked open the right door this time, and laid her purposefully down on the bed.

And prove it he did.

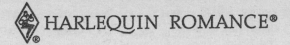

HARLEQUIN ROMANCE®

brings you

Stories that celebrate love, families and children!

Watch for our next Kids & Kisses title in October.

**Sullivan's Law
by Amanda Clark
Harlequin Romance #3333**

A warm, engaging Romance about people you'll love and a place that evokes rural America at its best. By the author of **A Neighborly Affair** *and* **Early Harvest.**

Jenny Carver is a single parent; she works too hard and worries too much. Her son, Chris, is a typical twelve-year-old—not quite a kid anymore but nowhere near adulthood. He's confused and bored and resentful—and Jenny isn't sure how to handle him. What she decides to do is take him to Tucker's Pond in Maine for the summer—a summer that changes both their lives. Especially when they meet a man named Ben Sullivan....

Available wherever Harlequin books are sold.

KIDS5

Where do you find hot Texas nights, smooth Texas charm and dangerously sexy cowboys?

Crystal Creek reverberates with the exciting rhythm of Texas. Each story features the rugged individuals who live and love in the Lone Star state.

"...Crystal Creek wonderfully evokes the hot days and steamy nights of a small Texas community...impossible to put down until the last page is turned."
—*Romantic Times*

Praise for Bethany Campbell's *The Thunder Rolls*

"Bethany Campbell takes the reader into the minds of her characters so surely...one of the best Crystal Creek books so far. It will be hard to top...."
—*Rendezvous*

"This is the *best* of the Crystal Creek series to date."
—*Affaire de Coeur*

Don't miss the next book in this exciting series. Look for GENTLE ON MY MIND by BETHANY CAMPBELL

Available in October wherever Harlequin books are sold.

THE VENGEFUL GROOM
Sara Wood

Legend has it that those married in Eternity's chapel are destined for a lifetime of happiness. But happiness isn't what Giovanni wants from marriage—it's revenge!

Ten years ago, Tina's testimony sent Gio to prison—for a crime he didn't commit. *Now* he's back in Eternity and looking for a bride. *Now* Tina is about to learn just how ruthless and disturbingly sensual Gio's brand of vengeance can be.

THE VENGEFUL GROOM, available in October from Harlequin Presents, is the fifth book in Harlequin's new cross-line series, **WEDDINGS, INC.** Be sure to look for the sixth book, **EDGE OF ETERNITY,** by Jasmine Cresswell (Harlequin Intrigue #298), coming in November.

WED5

MIRA™

The brightest star in women's fiction!

This October, reach for the stars and watch all your dreams come true with **MIRA BOOKS**.

HEATHER GRAHAM POZZESSERE
Slow Burn in October
An enthralling tale of murder and passion set against the dark and glittering world of Miami.

SANDRA BROWN
The Devil's Own in October
She made a deal with the devil...but she didn't bargain on losing her heart.

BARBARA BRETTON
Tomorrow & Always in November
Unlikely lovers from very different worlds...they had to cross time to find one another.

PENNY JORDAN
For Better For Worse in December
Three couples, three dreams—can they rekindle the love and passion that first brought them together?

The sky has no limit with **MIRA BOOKS**